Walking
with
Harry

Walking
with
Harry

John W. Winter

Matador
5 Weir Road
Kibworth Beauchamp
Leicester LE8 0LQ, UK
Tel: (+44) 116 279 2299
Fax: (+44) 116 279 2277
Email: books@troubador.co.uk
Web: www.troubador.co.uk/matador

ISBN 978 1848767 782

British Library Cataloguing in Publication Data.
A catalogue record for this book is available from the British Library.

Typeset in 11pt StempelGaramond Roman by Troubador Publishing Ltd, Leicester, UK

Matador is an imprint of Troubador Publishing Ltd

Printed and bound in the UK by TJ International, Padstow, Cornwall

To the many British and French friends that I've had the pleasure of meeting in 25 years of 'Anglo-French Walks.'

Cover photo by Danièle Lacourt

CONTENTS

PREFACE

'No self-respecting choir would dream of accepting people who can't sing so why should Thurston Ramblers accept people who can't walk? What we need is an admissions policy.'

Thus spake Mrs O.L. Jonstone, the club's formidable president and founder-member.

It was her subsequent proposal to audition aspiring members which brought Harry Birch, fine-weather walker and club comedian, into open and outspoken opposition.

How did such diametrically opposed characters manage to co-exist in one small rambling club? Largely because of the good humour and good sense of its members who don't take them too seriously and secretly enjoy their verbal sparring.

MUTINY IN THE RANKS

'There's only one fly in the ointment,' said Harry, leaning forward, 'she's called Jonstone, president and founder-member of Thurston Ramblers. Mrs Olive Lavinia Jonstone.'

I had just asked the barman of the Rose and Crown where Thurston Ramblers held their meetings. Harry had overheard me, introduced himself and suggested a quiet seat in the corner. He'd been a member three years and would answer all my questions. In fact, I never had the chance to ask any.

Fuelled by a second pint of Guinness, Harry told me that Mrs Jonstone – he preferred to call her O.L. – was one of the old school.

'She thinks walking purifies the soul. The longer and harder the walk, the greater your reward in heaven. She walks like a sergeant – major in the Light Infantry, straight as a ramrod and just about as fast. Makes me cringe. She retired from teaching four years ago. God knows what she was like in her prime.'

He himself was not what you'd call a keen walker.

'Me, I'm more of a social walker, enjoy the company, like a good laugh. You can keep your high level map and GPS bashes with forty pounds on your back and to hell with the weather. Not for Harry Birch thank you very much. Now O.L. ...'

He was back on his favourite topic.

'She's as tough as old boots, that one. Should have been born in the 19th century. I can just see her blazing a trail across Africa. She'd have scared the loin cloths off the natives, that's for sure. They'd have thought she was God Almighty. And she wouldn't have been in too much of a hurry to put them right.'

Harry was now in full spate.

'That's the trouble here, you see. O.L. always wants her own way. Tell you what, if it wasn't for me, she'd probably get it! Comes from a military family. Her father ran the Home Guard during the war. O.L. would run Thurston Ramblers the same way, given half a chance. Talk about Dad's Army, O.L.'s Army, that's what we'd be! I'll tell you this, she's the nearest thing in a skirt you'll ever see to Captain Mainwaring. She'd like nothing more than marching us up the Pennine Way, living off the land and sleeping rough. She'd really enjoy that. I tell you, there's a nasty sadistic streak in that woman. She's only happy when she's landed you knee-deep in a peat bog with a blizzard bending you in two. And then, you wouldn't believe it, she thinks she's doing you a favour!'

Getting this off his chest was giving Harry so much pleasure, I couldn't help smiling. But what he'd told me was just the build-up to his big announcement.

'You think I've been laying it on a bit thick, don't you. Well you'll soon see for yourself. It's the A.G.M. tonight and if O.L. runs true to form, she's bound to come up with some ridiculous idea. Whatever it is, I'll have her, you bet. Somebody's got to.'

Harry wiped away the froth from his third

Guinness, leaned forward and announced confidentially, 'My mate Bert's put me up for the committee!'

A. G. M.s to me are usually as charming as a day of drizzle on Kinder Scout. Not so this one. I was actually looking forward to it as I followed Harry upstairs and found a seat at the back of the room. There must have been about thirty people present. Harry seemed to know them all. He had a few words or a wave for everyone. At first, I found his bonhomie somewhat over the top until I remembered he was, after all, a candidate for the committee.

A sharp rap on the table silenced all voices – except Harry's.

'Thank you ladies and gentlemen ... Thank you Mr Birch,' came a high-pitched, authoritarian voice from the front, clearly that of the president. Mrs O.L. Jonstone was not the towering virago I had expected to see: she was, in fact, of medium height and slim build. What did impress me was her decisive manner. Here was a woman who would stand no nonsense. I began to think there might be a grain of truth in Harry's Guinness-fuelled indictment of O.L. For proof, I had to wait for item 5, 'Election of New Members.'

'I will come straight to the point,' announced the president, 'Thurston Ramblers needs an admissions policy. We need a clear-cut procedure to audition, as it were, aspiring members of this club. No self-respecting choir would dream of accepting people who can't sing so why should a club like Thurston Ramblers accept people who can't walk?'

I noticed several people, Harry among them, shuffling in their seats and exchanging glances at this interesting analogy. Spurred on, she continued.

'To be perfectly frank, we have enough stragglers as it is. We simply cannot allow any old Tom, Dick or Ha …'

She stopped abruptly but too late. The damage had been done. Spontaneous laughter erupted followed by wisecracks.

'Sounds like you're not wanted, Arry,' came one voice.

'Nay, be fair, it's only **old** Arries not wanted,' came another.

A third voice pointed out that Harry was no spring chicken whereupon someone else, obviously not a member of Harry's fan club, added that old or not, one Harry was enough.

O.L. forced a smile to her lips and restored order with a sharp

'Thank you. Thank you ladies and gentlemen. Nothing personal, I assure you.' Harry in turn assured her that no offence had been taken but I wasn't totally convinced.

'As I was saying,' she went on, 'we cannot allow just anyone to join our ranks. We do not exist for the benefit of people who amble twice round the park on a Sunday morning and then collapse onto a bench. May I remind you that we are ramblers not amblers, much less a refuge for geriatrics. Not that you need to be old to be geriatric. We all know some people in their forties who walk as if they have one foot in the grave.'

If the first reference to Harry was a Freudian slip, this one, accompanied by a glance in Harry's direction, was not. Ignoring the nudges and titters, O.L. continued.

'In conclusion, I propose that aspiring members of Thurston Ramblers be required to demonstrate both their physical fitness and their perseverance on a 15 mile hill and moorland walk in the company of two members of the committee and, of course, myself. We will assess their performance and recommend accordingly.'

'I second,' came an obviously primed voice from the front row.

There was a stunned silence. Just when O.L. was about to ask for all in favour, Harry begged leave to ask a question. This was the moment I had been waiting for, the promised confrontation. I couldn't have been more disappointed.

'What about the weather?' asked Harry innocently, looking as if butter wouldn't melt in his mouth. I wasn't the only one to be taken aback. O.L. herself, ready no doubt to meet broadside with broadside, could only splutter,

'Weather? Weather? What do you mean weather?'

'Well,' said Harry, meek as you please, 'suppose the weather for the test is sunny but not too hot with a nice cool breeze and good visibility.'

Here Harry paused as if his meaning was crystal clear and he didn't want to labour the point. O.L. hated obscurity. In a tone heavily overloaded with forbearance, she asked if Mr Birch would be kind enough to explain what he had in mind. Harry explained, slowly, weighing his words, perhaps a shade condescendingly.

'What I mean is that we cannot expect aspiring members to demonstrate their physical fitness and strength of will in ideal conditions. What we need is heavy rain or better still, driving snow, low cloud and fog. Conditions like these would show us what they're really made of, being wet, cold, exhausted and lost.'

Harry paused to let his point sink in before adding, still expressionless,

'That would weed out the amblers and the geriatrics, don't you think?'

A puzzled expression had settled on O.L.'s face. Whose side was Harry on? Could he have seen the light at last? Finally, she gave him the benefit of the doubt. Smiling sweetly, she pointed out that much as she approved of his – rather unexpected sentiments – she could hardly guarantee the most suitable weather for each test walk.

Harry looked thoughtful. 'You're right of course,' he went on, 'To be absolutely fair, each candidate would have to be tested in similar weather – similar foul weather of course. I suppose we'd just have to wait for the weather to oblige.'

O.L. frowned once more but Harry gave her no time to reply.'Got it! Cracked it! We tell candidates to stand by the phone every Sunday morning at 07.30 until the weather's right – or wrong, if you see what I mean. They would have to be kitted out, ready to leave as soon as you rang. Same thing for the two committee members – and yourself of course.'

By this time, O.L. had had enough. 'Really Mr Birch, I've never heard such nonsense. On that basis, we'd never get any new members at all.'

Harry smiled broadly. 'My sentiments exactly, madam president.'

He was just about to sit down when he changed his

mind. 'Hold on, I've thought of another possibility. What about hiring the Commando assault course just outside town? It would be much easier to organise. You could stipulate three times round on a sunny day or twice in foul weather.'

From the hoots of laughter that followed, O.L. salvaged what dignity she could. 'If Mr Birch chooses to be facetious, I see no point in discussing the matter further.'

Harry won his second victory later when he was elected to the committee. As for me, I joined the club there and then. It promised to be fun.

HARRY'S MYSTERY WALK

Harry Birch was basically a fine weather walker. Comfortably settled into his mid-forties, he felt no compelling urge to tread where no man had trod before. Nor had he any intention of pushing himself anywhere near the threshold of human endurance. Easy-going, generous, the life and soul of the party, he was a popular member of the club. Unmarried, working at home on computers, a member of the local dramatic society and a keen photographer, he really enjoyed his outings with Thurston Ramblers in spite of his disapproval of the president, Mrs O.L.Jonstone.

O.L. was none too fond of Harry either. To her, he was not a serious walker. What's more, she considered him a subversive element in the club. At the A.G.M. he had openly challenged her authority and even made fun of her proposal for an admissions policy. She had been appalled by his election to the committee, not least because it was customary for all members of the committee to lead a walk during their year of office.

The thought of a walk led by Harry Birch filled O.L. with dismay. It was bound to be low-level; probably meandering across farm land on field paths or worse, walking on tarmac. There would be no breathtaking views, no challenging paths, no sense of achievement. She doubted if they would even break sweat. To this dismal prospect, O.L. had ruefully resigned herself. The walk she herself was proposing to lead to Scafell Pike would more than compensate: the mere thought of it made her blood tingle. Harry Birch would chicken out of that for sure.

When the annual programme appeared, O.L.'s disapproval of Harry reached a new low. 'Sunday February 5. **Mystery Tour.** Leader: Harry Birch. Meet Ploughman's Arms 10 a.m.' O.L. bristled at the vagueness of the title. She liked to know where she was going and she trusted nobody else's route-finding to get there, least of all Harry's.

'Mystery Tour indeed,' she muttered to Gladys, 'Just an excuse for getting lost.'

Meeting at a pub didn't please her either. Harry's fondness for Guinness was well known and even though the pub would be closed, she was uneasy about meeting there. As for the 10 a.m. start, this was a flagrant flouting of tradition: Thurston Ramblers were always off at the latest by 9 a.m. – 8 a.m. or even earlier in the summer.

It wasn't a bad day for February. There was a sprinkling of snow on the ground and a nip in the air. Some patchy cloud gave a hint that the sun might break through.

'Waste of a promising day,' hissed O.L. to Gladys as they arrived at the Ploughman's Arms. 'Pussyfooting round with Harry Birch when we could be doing Ingleborough or Pen-y-ghent.'

Gladys said nothing. Seventy plus, a steady walker, cheerful but accident prone, she was secretly pleased to forego slogging up Ingleborough or Pen-y-ghent.

By 10 a.m., sixteen members had assembled on the

car park but Harry was not among them. Unpunctuality to O.L. was a cardinal sin. Irresponsibility was another. Harry was guilty of both. Five minutes later, just when she was about to announce the alternative walk she had prepared, a side door opened and out of the pub stepped Harry, unrepentant and cheerful as ever.

After gracefully acknowledging the ironic cheers, he addressed the group.

'Ladies and gentlemen, welcome one and all. The first stop on our mystery tour is here at the Ploughman's Arms. Mine host, and very good friend, has concocted, with a little help from yours truly, an excellent bowl of punch. Not only that, he has kindly put at our disposal his private parlour complete with log fire.' With a histrionic flourish, he concluded, 'A stirrup cup, ladies and gentlemen, ere we plod on to pastures new.'

O.L. was speechless. Never in the history of Thurston Ramblers had a walk begun in a pub. Seeking support, she looked round for Mike and Joe, the club's hard men, pacemakers and trail-blazers like herself. But only their backs could be seen as the whole group surged forward, carrying her with it. Bundled into the pub, she had to accept defeat. Concealing her fury as best she could, she managed to muster a weak smile as Harry thrust into her hand a glass of steaming punch, destined to find its way to the aspidistra near the door when no-one was looking.

The scene in the over-crowded, over-heated parlour did nothing to lighten her mood. Discarded fleeces and anoraks littered tables and chairs. Harry, exuding bonhomie, was topping up glasses, urging everyone to have one more for the road. Gladys kept informing anyone who might be listening that her legs already felt like jelly. Penny, whose main motive in joining the club was to lose weight, was overlapping a fireside chair, nursing the pub cat, both purring with contentment. Bert, plumber by trade and comedian by nature, was telling some of his risqué jokes to the shocked delight of the young primary school teachers Mavis and Betty. No-one showed the slightest inclination to move.

To O.L., the situation had become critical. The moral fibre of Thurston Ramblers was being sapped away by a virus of epidemic proportions, spread by that lay-about Harry Birch. At 10.25, she forced her way through to Harry and enquired acidly when he proposed to start his walk. Harry downed what remained in the punchbowl, consulted his watch and called for order.

'Ladies and gentlemen, the open road awaits. Our bus will arrive in five minutes. It will stop just outside the pub.'

A barrage of questions followed. 'The bus?' 'What bus?' 'Where are we going, Harry? 'What have you hatched up now, Harry?'

To all of which, Harry replied, 'That, my friends, is surprise number two.'

Twenty minutes later, the party debussed at an isolated crossroads, high on the moors. A blustery wind had sprung up, bringing with it black clouds and a threat of more snow. Ignoring such trivia, O.L. scanned the horizon. The only feature offering any sort of challenge was a snow-covered ridge about a mile away, rising steeply across rough grassland. Assuming this to be their objective and not wishing to squander any more time, she set off at a brisk pace until Harry called her back. He was pointing out a cart-track running horizontally towards a plantation.

O.L., Mike and Joe took up their usual positions at the front. Harry, like the Duke of Plaza Torro, preferred to lead from the rear: he found it more sociable. Ambling along with Mavis and Betty, it wasn't long before he had lost sight of the front runners. Not that this worried him: he knew they would have to wait where the track forked beyond the plantation.

O.L. hated having to wait for stragglers. But her eyes lit up at the fork when she saw a narrow path on the left curling up the hillside which would, she supposed, lead to the snow-capped ridge. At least, Harry's mystery tour wouldn't be a complete fiasco. Unable to stand still, she marched down the track to demand directions.

'Are we right or left at the fork?' she shouted when Harry came into view.

'I don't know,' was Harry's reply.

O.L. spluttered in disbelief. How could the man be so brazenly irresponsible?

'We won't know till we get there and toss up,' continued Harry.

Nervous titters came from Gladys who sensed that the cold war between the two was in imminent danger of becoming hot. Calmly, Harry pointed out that the whole idea of a mystery tour was not knowing where you were going.

At the fork, Harry spun a coin.

'Heads we go right, tails we go left.' The coin showed heads.

'Pity,' said Harry, poker-faced, 'that path up there on the left looks very inviting.'

Penny, who didn't realise he was joking, consoled him by saying that anyway the wind would be in their backs and that walking downhill was easier than going up. Unable to conceal her disappointment, O.L. stalked off to the right, muttering how idiotic it was to organise a walk on the toss of a coin.

It was on the way down through the quarry that Gladys had one of her accidents when she fell and turned her ankle. Those near by were sympathetic but not surprised: Gladys was not the most sure-footed of walkers. Refusing to be fussed over, she said she would walk it off and insisted on continuing.

At the bottom of the quarry, O.L. was getting impatient. Binoculars focussed on the stragglers, she realised at once the reason for the hold up.

'It's Gladys again. She's had another fall. I really think she should call it a day. It was blisters at Malham, a sprained wrist in Nidderdale and her knee gave way coming down Whernside. Come to think of it, those glasses of punch she had wouldn't improve her balance either.'

Flurries of snow were dancing in the air and the sky was looking ominous when Gladys and her escorts rejoined the group. Gladys did her best not to hold them back but progress was slow and people were stamping their feet and rubbing their hands to keep warm. When the path forked again, O.L. enquired if Mr Birch would be kind enough to indicate their direction.

'No problem,' replied Harry, producing his coin which again came down heads.

The path on the right followed a stream into a thinly wooded valley. It was snowing steadily now and about time they thought of eating. O.L. proposed sending scouts ahead to look for shelter

'Just a minute,' cried Harry, 'I can see a road over there. Suppose we make for it and see what fate has in store for us. You never know, there could be a pub by the roadside.'

They weren't sorry to reach the tarmac. Out came the coin again.

'Heads it's right, tails it's left.' said Harry. Heads it was.

'Great,' he cried, 'I do believe there's a pub ten minutes away. Somebody up there is on our side, that's for sure.'

This news was received so enthusiastically that O.L. was left standing at the start. Equally unusual was the sight of Harry at the front.

'He's like a hound that's scented a fox,' said Mavis.

'Actually,' said Betty, 'I think it's the Guinness he's scented.'

Even Gladys quickened her pace. It had dawned on her that not only were they heading for the warmth and shelter of a pub but that by invariably turning right, they had been walking in a circle. They couldn't be far from their starting point.

Like the Ploughman's Arms, the Grapes of Wrath offered Thurston Ramblers a warm welcome. A log fire was blazing in the snug and the landlord, who, oddly enough, was on Christian name terms with Harry, wasn't at all put out by the puddles of melted snow and dripping anoraks. Anyone might have thought he was expecting them. Harry announced that home-made chicken soup was on offer and that he personally could recommend the draught Guinness.

During lunch, O.L. mellowed. The hot soup, the crackling logs and the good spirits of the group made her forget, temporarily at least, her earlier clashes with Harry as she chatted with Gladys. Harry and Syd had challenged Mike and Joe to a game of darts; Bert was teaching Mavis how to play pool and Penny had found another cat to stroke. When O.L. finally looked at her watch, she couldn't believe it; they must have been in the pub almost two hours. She asked Harry in an unusually mild voice,

'We're not staying here all day, are we?'

'Unfortunately not,' Harry replied, 'the pub will be closing soon. Mind you, I can't think of a better place to be snowbound. Actually, I have it on good authority that a bus passes this pub in ten minutes. Or, of course, we could always walk back to the cars; it'll only take forty minutes, maybe fifty what with Gladys limping and all this snow. Suppose I toss for it.'

It was an unnecessary question and Harry knew it. A chorus of voices told him not to bother.

Sitting next to Harry on the bus, Gladys enthused about the events of the day. In spite of her swollen ankle, she had enjoyed herself.

'That punch put me just in the right frame of mind for a mystery tour. I loved walking along the plantation and what a good thing we didn't have to climb up to that snowy ridge. We might still be there now, floundering about in snow drifts. You were really lucky with that coin, weren't you. We would have missed this bus and that lovely pub if we'd turned left instead of right when we got to the road.'

Harry smiled. 'Actually, Gladys, just between you and me, luck didn't come into it. When the forecast said it would snow today, it was just a matter of re-jigging my original route, checking bus time-tables and phoning two pubs to let them know what we wanted.'

'But the route we took, it all depended on the toss of a coin,' said Gladys. Harry moved closer. 'Not any old coin, this particular coin, Gladys. See, it's double-headed. Bought it at a joke shop years ago. I knew it would come in handy some day.'

BETTY'S FOREST OF BOWLAND WALK

Harry was feeling pleased with himself. The sun was already shining and the prospect of a none too strenuous walk in the Hodder valley was very appealing. Particularly since Betty had let slip they'd be picnicking near a pub around lunch-time. So why bother with a picnic, thought Harry. There would be less weight in his bag and a liquid lunch at a pub was much more civilised than an alfresco picnic.

Harry was well aware that O.L. would pour scorn on such an idea. Picnics were the norm and anyway, she thought pub lunches during a walk were a waste of time and money. But eating alone held no attraction for Harry. Maybe young Mavis, who always laughed at his jokes, could be persuaded to join him. Or maybe Gladys, who tended to keep a motherly eye on him: she would keep him up to date with the latest gossip.

There was another thing Harry was pleased about. He had arranged for his pal Bert to meet him at the lunch-time pub that morning. Harry would leave his car there and Bert would take him to the starting point of the walk on his motorbike. Asked why, Harry said it was always a good idea to have transport available, you never knew when it might come in handy. But would Bert kindly keep quiet about it. O.L. would certainly disapprove: she would think having a car half-way might tempt some to abandon the full walk. Bert acquiesced grinning. He knew very well that if anyone might want to cut short a walk, it would be Harry.

Bert's arrival in the car park at Dunsop Bridge on his motorbike with Harry perched on the pillion, caused a sensation. Harry acknowledged the cheers with both arms in the air as if he'd scored the winning goal in the cup final. No, his car had not broken down; he had just felt like a breath of fresh air that's all.

Betty counted her group. 18, not a bad turn-out for a day in early March although the weather couldn't be better: blue sky, sun and just a light breeze. At 35, Betty was plump, bright and breezy. She loved teaching but was always glad to forget about children at weekends. Today would be hassle-free. Or would it? Sometimes adults could be more trying than kids. O.L, for example, was already champing at the bit, irritated by the time it took Harry and Bert to put on their boots.

The first delay occurred when they were walking through the village.

'Oo, look at the ducks,' squealed Mavis as a score of mallards left the stream and came waddling towards them.

Two of the ladies delved into their bags and decided they had one sandwich too many. Mavis and several others thought the scene worth a photograph.

'You'd think ducks were an endangered species,' growled O.L.

Delay number two occurred immediately after the ducks had been fed and photographed. Gladys, looking at the window of the post office-cum-general store-cum café, had spotted something which she felt all present should be told about.

'Did you know we are, according to the Ordnance Survey, at this very moment, at the exact centre of Great Britain? Look, there's a postcard with it on'

By the time half the group had bought the postcard, thirty minutes had passed and they had not walked more than 150 yards. O.L. was seething.

'For goodness sake, Betty, exert some authority,' she barked, 'We haven't come here just to feed ducks, take photos and buy postcards.'

Betty marshalled her troops with some difficulty but just as they were crossing the bridge, someone called out, 'Where's Joyce?' It wasn't the first time Joyce had disappeared on a walk. Everyone knew she had a weak bladder. Given time, she would re-appear from behind a bush. But here, there were no bushes. Someone suggested that she must have gone back to the public toilets in the car park. O.L.'s impatience had now reached fever pitch. When Joyce eventually appeared, O.L. marched forward to reprimand her.

'You've kept us all waiting again. Why can't you get your timing right? You could have gone when we arrived at the car park.'

Joyce pointed out that it was a good half hour since they left the car park and when the urge came …. O.L.. wasn't listening. Striding back to the bridge, she rejoined Betty at the head of the group.

Betty's walk took them along a pleasant lane to a footbridge and on past a farm which specialised in breeding pheasants. Here another delay might have occurred had O.L. not stationed herself in front of the enclosure and waved everyone on like a policeman directing traffic. In the next field, however, she had to admit defeat. Lambs! Another photo opportunity not to be missed.

'Bugger!' There was no mistaking Harry's voice. While moving up to take a photo of a ewe with twin lambs, he had gone ankle-deep in a cow pat. The reactions from those near by were predictable: raucous guffaws from his pal Bert, giggles from Penny, sympathy from Gladys and outrage from O.L.

'Mr Birch! Really! Do you have to resort to such language? With ladies present, it won't do. I think an apology is called for.'

Gladys, the peace-maker, suggested that he really meant beggar but Harry vehemently denied any such confusion.

'Bugger or beggar, you can take your pick, Gladys. Just think yourself lucky it wasn't worse. Bleeding cows! They've this whole field to shit in and they choose to foul up the path. Farmers should be made to put nappies on them.'

This triggered another fit of giggles from Penny but O.L, not amused, strode on.

After a short stretch of road, the group headed south and her spirits revived when she saw the path ahead leading steeply up a hill. Consulting her map, she announced, 'Mellor Knoll, 344 metres. Real walking at last.'

Harry was the last to get to the top of the hill. Betty had asked him to be back marker, knowing he would be last in any case. Penny plodded along with him, keeping up a constant flow of chatter and oblivious to the splendid views of the Hodder Valley below and the fells beyond.

When Betty called a halt for elevenses, O.L. saw no reason to stop, saying they had already had their break in Dunsop Bridge. Gladys, however, among others, was beginning to struggle so Betty stuck to her guns and announced a ten minute pause. Joyce too was glad of the opportunity to disappear discreetly into the wood near by. Harry handed round a packet of Jaffa cakes in response to the dried apricots and figs offered by O.L.

'Downhill all the way now,' shouted Betty, as the group moved off.

'We've heard that one before,' retorted Harry, before asking casually how long it would take to get to the pub. Betty reckoned about an hour and a half, if all went well. Way-finding wasn't too obvious but Betty navigated confidently through another wood, along tracks and lanes and past several farms. The notice nailed on one farm gate caused some amusement, 'Never mind the dog, beware of the wife.' Syd was heard to remark that he'd like one like that for his own garden gate.

From a hill further on, the river came into view again.

'Not far now to our picnic spot by the pub,' said Betty encouragingly to those who were lagging behind, 'Just down this slope and across the stepping stones.'

The mention of stepping stones alarmed Gladys. Not sure-footed at the best of times, when tired she was even less so. Harry chivalrously tried to reassure her by saying he would hold her hand. When they reached the stepping stones, Gladys was even more alarmed to see that the river was in spate and some stones were under water. She watched apprehensively as, one by one, the others inched their way over. Harry, none too happy himself, put on a brave face.

'Come on Gladys, you can do it. I'll go first and hold your hand.' The crossing seemed to take for ever. Gladys's progress was painfully slow as she clung like a leech to Harry. She tottered several times but managed to stay upright until the last few stones. It was probably applause from the waiting group which caused her to lose concentration, wobble, lose balance completely and fall in. By some miracle, Harry managed not to follow her.

It could have been worse. At that point, the river was only knee deep and helped by Harry, Gladys was able to stumble to the bank. Typically, she brushed aside commiserations: she would be fine after a few minutes rest and why didn't they all get on with their picnics. Harry too was a bit shaken but not too shaken to forget about the pub lunch he'd anticipated.

'Now then, Gladys,' he said, 'what you need right now is a change of boots, socks and trousers. I've a pair of flip-flops in my car and some socks in my bag; waterproof over-trousers too if you can get into them. I suggest we go straight up to the pub. While you're getting changed, I'll order two bowls of soup. What do you say?'

Gladys nodded. She didn't like being fussed over but she was shivering and Harry seemed to know what was best. O.L. had admired the way he had helped Gladys over the stepping stones and now his practical suggestions met with her approval. But she had pricked up her ears at Harry's mention of a car and asked if he'd forgotten he'd come on Bert's motorbike.

'Well,' replied Harry, unable to suppress a smile, 'as

a matter of fact, I left my car at the pub car park and Bert gave me a lift from there. I had a premonition it might come in handy. I don't think Gladys is in any fit state to walk back to Dunsop Bridge so the car will be handy, don't you think.'

O.L. could only agree in spite of Gladys protesting that she would be perfectly able to complete the walk after a change and some hot soup. Harry would have none of it: after a fall like that, she needed time to recover. Besides, he knew for a fact that the path back was very rough and wet in parts. She wouldn't want another fall, would she. It would slow the whole group down and there could be a problem getting her to the car. Reluctantly, Gladys agreed and they both set off to the pub leaving the others to picnic by the river.

'Pity you'll miss the walk back, Harry,' called Bert as they were leaving, 'if you like, you could leave Gladys at the pub, finish the walk with us and I'll bring you back on the bike to collect her.'

Harry said he wouldn't dream of leaving Gladys alone and even if it did mean he would have to miss the afternoon walk, so be it. As an afterthought, he added that the tea shop in Dunsop Bridge would be a convenient meeting place at, say, about 4 o'clock.

O.L. viewed Harry's magnanimous gesture of self-sacrifice with suspicion. It wouldn't be the first time he'd conjured up some reason for not finishing a walk. The very fact that he'd left his car at the pub suggested an ulterior motive. On the other hand, he couldn't possibly have foreseen that Gladys would fall in the river. Maybe, even without her accident, he had hatched another plot to justify absconding. He was a devious one, that Harry Birch.

On the whole, the morning's walk had dissatisfied her. Too much shilly-shallying, too many unnecessary stops, no real challenge. The prospect of the walk back along the river didn't inspire her either. Thinking Mike and Joe would feel the same, she called them over. Suppose the three of them were to add a few miles to the afternoon walk and go back over Birkett Fell. They wouldn't have to wait every five minutes for the rest to catch up and the climb would get the blood circulating at last.

When Mike and Joe agreed, O.L. asked Betty if she would have any objection to her group being further reduced. Betty, always accommodating, saw no objection. There would now be 13 for the homeward stretch. Losing the two slowest in Harry and Gladys and the three fastest in O.L., Mike and Joe had an advantage: her group would no longer be spread out over half a mile or more. She wouldn't have to urge on the tortoises or restrain the hares. It would make life easier for her.

Harry's leisurely liquid lunch in the company of Gladys, fully recovered and cheerful as ever was followed by a very agreeable drive through the Forest of Bowland and afternoon tea with the re-united group. Everything, including the weather, had turned out well. The group had awarded him brownie points for looking after Gladys and possibly, just possibly, he had gone up a tad in O.L.'s estimation.

JOE'S LAKELAND WALK

'I did the recce last Wednesday and I almost came to grief on Dore Screes.'

Joe was talking to members of the club who had assembled in the room at the Rose and Crown where they met every fortnight to discus walks past and walks to come, show photos and slides, have quizzes, listen to talks and drink coffee or, in Harry's case, Guinness.

Pint in hand, Harry had just arrived as Joe was talking about next Sunday's walk, the Mosedale Horseshoe from Wasdale Head. His immediate thought was that if Joe, one of the club's hard men, had almost come to grief there, the Mosedale Horseshoe wasn't for him. O.L. was of the same opinion.

'Not your cup of tea, this one, Harry,' she said, trying not very successfully to give the impression that she would miss him. '800 metres of climbing up to Pillar, rocky descent to Wind Gap, a bit of scrambling up to Little Scoat Fell, over Red Pike and down Dore Screes into Mosedale.'

With a rare twinkle in her eye, she added,

'Mind you there's a lovely pub at the finish. After all that effort, you'd really enjoy your Guinness.'

Harry smiled and bided his time.

Joe had said that the descent down Dore Screes was very steep and slippery. In wet weather it could even be lethal. Twice he'd lost his footing. For once he found himself wishing he had a stick. His words set off alarm bells for Gladys.

'You're surely not taking us down there, Joe?' she exclaimed, 'I'd never make it!.'

When several others echoed her fears, Joe reassured them. He'd studied the map and there was an easier way down. Instead of going on to Red Pike, they could go down to Scoat Tarn and join the path coming from Haycock. Then there was a long, gradual descent of about three miles following Nether Beck to the Wasdale road.

'Just as a matter of interest, how far would the pub be from there?' asked Harry to the surprise of O.L. who had already written him off.

'Well,' said Joe, 'from Netherbeck Bridge, it's a good two miles of road walking back to the Wasdale Inn. What I suggest is that we leave a car at the bridge. That way, drivers could be taken back to pick up their cars and then return to collect the rest of the group.'

Harry wanted clarification. 'Hold on Joe. We get to Netherbeck Bridge, wait maybe twenty minutes for the drivers to come back from the pub in their cars then what? Head for home or double back to the pub for food and drink?'

O.L. got in first. 'I can't think why you need bother your head about that, Mr Birch. I doubt very much if we'll have the pleasure of your company on Sunday. For myself, I would not approve of going back to the pub. It would take at least an hour to get there and for all of us to be served and the journey home, as you know, takes at least two hours. As it is, I'd be surprised if we were back by 8.'

To pour oil on troubled waters, Gladys asked if the decision could not be made on the spot; if they got down early enough, maybe they would have time to go back to the pub.It would be nice to have something to eat before setting off. Besides, she was sure the toilets would be appreciated.

Joe agreed and then went on to talk about the route. It would mean an early start at 07.30. He wasn't too keen on the shortest route over Wrynose Pass and Hardknott Pass; the road was steep, mostly single track and there were some very awkward hair-pin bends. Better and probably quicker to take the coast road via Ravenglass. They should get to Wasdale Head about 9.30, leave a car at Netherbeck Bridge and be ready for off by 10. It was a lovely stroll up the eastern slopes of Mosedale for the first mile then the path steepened as it approached Black Sail Pass. He thought there would be about 500 metres of ascent up to that point.

O.L. was getting impatient. She had been looking forward to doing the classic Mosedale Horseshoe, Red Pike, Dore Screes and all. The descent Joe had proposed via Scoat Tarn was a soft option, a concession to the faint-hearted. Still, there was one consolation, Harry Birch wouldn't be there to slow them down. Nor, she hoped, would Gladys. Plucky and cheerful she might be, Gladys was an accident waiting to happen. It was high time she realised her limitations.

O.L. had done her homework. She knew almost word for word what her hero Mr Wainwright – she always called him 'Mr' as a mark of respect – had to say about the path up to Pillar. Interrupting Joe, she wanted to know if they would be doing the High Level Traverse to Pillar Rock. When Joe said they would, always providing decent weather, she was clearly much relieved: she beamed at all around, including Harry who appeared oddly preoccupied.

On the morning of the walk, the arrival of Harry in the car-park, accompanied by Gladys, astounded O.L.

'What are you two doing here?' she spluttered.

'Why not?' laughed Harry. 'It's a grand morning and the pub you mentioned sounds very fetching. Actually, I'm going to do you a favour. You won't have to bother taking a car back to Netherbeck Bridge when we get to Wasdale Head. I'll be there when you get down with mine. Now what about hitting the road? O.K. Joe?'

There were 12 in the group and 4 cars, including Harry's. On the drive up the M6, O.L. tried to figure out what exactly he had in mind. If he was going to meet them at the finish, he couldn't be planning to do the walk; that was a relief, anyway. But why, when they finally arrived at the Wasdale Inn, was Harry putting his boots on? Gladys too. This was a serious walk for serious walkers. She tried to quiz Harry on his intentions but he didn't give much away.

'First things first,' was all the reply he made. 'I think a coffee in the pub is called for after that long drive.' Everybody, with one exception, thought this a good idea. O.L. said she would wait outside.

By the time they had all emerged from the pub, Joe had been to look at the local weather forecast pinned up at the outdoor shop. Looking rather worried, he announced,

'Cloud base 600 metres, squally showers, occasional sunny periods.'

The views round about were not encouraging. Lingmell and Kirk Fell summits were invisible as was all the upper Mosedale valley.

'Too bright, too early,' said Joe, 'It's time for a rethink. For starters, we can forget about the High Level Traverse: we'd be in cloud and slithering about on wet rock would be asking for trouble. We'd be all right up to Black Sail Pass but obviously Pillar will be in cloud and we'd be in cloud for another hour until we got to Scoat Tarn. Sorry, Olive, it's just not on.'

O.L. was hugely disappointed at having to miss the High Level Traverse but the possibility of aborting Pillar was unthinkable. She said she hadn't come all this way to be put off by cloud and the chance of a few showers; that's what one expected in the Lakes. They were all, well nearly all, with a glance in the direction of Harry, experienced walkers, they all had waterproofs and anyway, the forecast talked about sunny periods so why didn't they just get moving.

Joe looked round to gauge the general feeling. There was a lot of shuffling of feet and shrugging of shoulders. Harry said nothing. He didn't need to; everyone knew what his opinion would be. Finally, to break the stalemate, Joe suggested they take it stage by stage: when they got to Black Sail Pass, they could decide whether to go on to Pillar. If and when they got there, they would have to decide whether to continue as planned or retrace their steps.

This plan placated O.L. and was thought sensible by the rest of the group. Whatever Harry thought, he didn't say. In no hurry to set off, he was busy taking photos, one of Gladys and Penny outside the inn, another of Joyce emerging from the toilet and a third of the group, led by Joe and O.L., crossing the footbridge.

Harry enjoyed the first mile: the gradient was gentle and there were pleasant views up the lower Mosedale valley. Gladys, Penny and he were inevitably at the rear but when Joe paused to regroup, he and O.L. didn't have too long to wait.

'You're on form this morning, Harry,' called Bert, 'Joined a keep fit class or what?'

'Not exactly,' Harry replied, poker-faced, 'But I had a work-out in the gym on Thursday. That rowing machine they've got, I can really recommend it for keeping the flab at bay. Lost two pounds in one session. Came out fit as a butcher's dog.'

This was a revelation. Mavis asked if he didn't mean 'fat as a butcher's dog.' Bert said that's how he went in but frankly he couldn't see much difference today. O.L. couldn't believe her ears. Harry Birch on a rowing machine? He was surely winding them up. Yet a nagging doubt persisted. She had to admit that he had kept up better than usual so far. Maybe, at long last, he had seen the light. The next 400 metres up to the pass would show how fit he really was.

The path above Gatherstone Beck, with the western slopes of Kirk Fell soaring upwards on the right, became steeper and stonier as the group grew nearer the pass. O.L.'s spirits rose with each step. She was in her element. This was the kind of walking that gave her a buzz. By now, the others were well strung out and the visibility had deteriorated. In the mist, she could just make out Harry, Gladys and Penny.

She and Joe would have to wait at least five minutes for them at the pass. But the very fact that Harry was still plodding upwards surprised her. Never in the past three years had he climbed more than 300 metres and today, assuming he reached the pass, he would have done 500.

When Harry, Gladys and Penny did get to the pass, they sank to the ground, exhausted as cloud swirled round them, driven by a brisk wind coming up from Ennerdale. O.L. and Joe had already put on their anoraks, over-trousers, hats and gloves: the others followed their example. After drinks and snacks Joe gathered them all together to discuss stage two.

'Well, it's decision time,' he announced. 'It's taken us just over an hour and a half to get here so we're O.K. for time. The critical factor is the weather. I'd say visibility at the moment is about 20 yards but it'll almost certainly get worse higher up. What do you think?'

O.L. was all for pressing on, repeating the view she'd expressed earlier that she hadn't come all this way to be thwarted by low cloud. Besides, the forecast had said there would be occasional sunny periods; the summit might well be swathed in blue sky and sunshine.

'And pigs might fly,' muttered Harry.

He had no intention, had never had the intention, of going beyond Black Sail Pass. To have got so far was, in itself, an achievement. Let the others go ahead if they wished, he would go down, enjoy a hot meal at the inn and then meet them as promised at Netherbeck Bridge. Gladys, Penny and Joyce also decided that enough was enough and the four of them set off on the descent as the other nine disappeared upwards into the cloud.

It was about 40 minutes later that O.L.'s optimism began to seem justified: a break in the cloud revealed a watery sun behind them as they were nearing the summit. There were smiles all round, not least from O.L., basking in the knowledge that her judgement had been vindicated. It was a sudden shout from Joe that stopped them in their tracks. With the sun on his back, he was looking downwards into the cloud and pointing at his magnified shadow with a halo round his head.

'It's the Brocken spectre,' he cried, as the others gathered round him. 'The name comes from a peak in the Harz mountains where the phenomenon was first observed in the early 19th century.' O.L. had read about it. Now seeing her own shadow with its halo of coloured rings, she couldn't conceal her delight. She would dine out on this occasion for years to come. Bert took a photo of her ghostly figure outlined against the cloud; although blurred, it was recognisably O.L. What a pity Harry was not with them. Still, when he saw the photo of O.L. beatified, he would surely have some interesting comments to make.

It was after the final rocky climb, still in sunshine, to the summit of Pillar that a second surprise awaited them. They could see the tops of the Scafell range piercing the white cotton-wool cloud below them. It was another magical moment. O.L. was cock-a-hoop. Exhilaration had now replaced her disappointment at missing out on the High Level Traverse. She hadn't imagined such rare compensations as the Brocken spectre and the aerial view of the Scafell tops bathed in sunlight. Joe didn't completely share her euphoria. He kept looking up at the sky as they walked over the plateau, at O.L.'s insistence, to take a look at the formidable Pillar Rock.

Back at the primitive wind shelter, as flasks and sandwiches were being brought out, Joe announced that a leisurely lunch was out of the question. Gusts of wind were already bringing drops of rain and thick, dark clouds were threatening to obscure the sun at any moment. It only took a few minutes for the sky to darken. Swirling cloud and driving rain brought visibility down to ten yards. It was decision time again but this time Joe didn't ask for opinions. He knew exactly what had to be done.

'We're going to abort the horseshoe and go back the way we came up,' he stated. 'The descent to Wind Gap is steep and stony, there's some scrambling over Little Stoat Fell and the path round Scoat Tarn is sure to be waterlogged. In difficult conditions like these, apart from the problem of way-finding, we don't want to risk an accident. Even retracing our steps will be tricky enough: we'll all have to be very careful and, above all, keep close together. Keep no more than three yards apart and if you should lose sight of the person in front of you, shout loud and clear: in which case, everyone stops to regroup. Would you bring up the rear, Olive?'

This was a shrewd move on Joe's part. He knew very well how difficult it would be to restrain O.L. if, as always, she was striding ahead. In the circumstances, O.L. could hardly refuse his request. Being tail-end Charlie was an affront to her dignity as president and founder member of the club but she managed to swallow her pride and nodded.

The group followed Joe as he slowly picked his way

down through the slippery rocks. Now and again, the visibility improved a little but the rain, driven by strong gusts of wind made progress painfully slow. It was young Mavis who suffered most. The others all had more or less waterproof anoraks and over trousers; Mavis had a flimsy cape which billowed out leaving her exposed below the waist and also upset her balance. She stumbled several times and would have fallen headlong if O.L., not normally tolerant of human frailty, had not held her arm and encouraged her. According to Harry, Mavis brought out O.L.'s long submerged maternal instinct.

It took about ninety minutes to get down to the comparative security of Black Sail Pass where the cloud had thinned and the path down to Wasdale was more straightforward. Up to then, no-one had given a thought to Harry and the three ladies who had gone down with him. It now occurred to Bert that Harry was supposed to meet them at Netherbeck Bridge at the end of the planned walk. He wouldn't know they were coming down to Wasdale.

O.L. was not unduly concerned with Harry's plight.

'He'll have a long wait if he's gone there to meet us,' she almost chuckled, 'but my bet is that we'll find him in the pub, warming himself by the fire with a pint of Guinness in his hand.'

Mention of Harry and the pub put new life into Mavis. 'I can't wait to join him.' she cried, 'I'm soaked from the waist down, I've got wet feet, I'm cold and I'm hungry. Let's get a move on.' O.L. needed no second invitation. Abandoning her role as back-marker which she deemed no longer necessary, she shepherded Mavis to the front and set the pace. Joe accepted this with resignation, relieved to have got the group down so far without mishap. By the time they reached the pub, the rain had stopped and it looked as if another sunny period was imminent.

O.L.'s prediction was right again. There was Harry sitting by the fire, Guinness in hand surrounded by Gladys, Penny and Joyce.

'I see you've got wet,' said Harry grinning smugly.

'We're not as wet as some I could mention' snapped O.L., adding, as she stalked off towards the Ladies, 'Actually, you don't know what you've missed. We've had a most interesting walk.'

Bert, who had been fiddling with his digital camera, thought this an opportune moment to show Harry his photo. 'Just have a look at this, Harry, O.L. with a halo round her head. Just like one of the saints.' Harry perused the photo for some time. He had never heard of the Brocken spectre and Bert had to assure him that the photo was genuine.

'Well,' he said at last, 'I don't know how or where you took this, Bert, but I can't say I'm much surprised. Our dear President always thinks she's on the side of the angels. I dare say she takes this as confirmation. I suppose we ought to call her Saint Olive from now on … put her crazy ideas down to divine guidance … go down on bended knee and seek pardon for daring to disagree with her.'

These suggestions were met with laughter but not taken seriously. It was no secret that Harry and O.L. did not see eye to eye; nor that Harry enjoyed playing the role of agent provocateur.

When O.L. came back, stripped of her wet gear, she recounted to Gladys, Penny and Joyce the day's adventures in vivid detail. They had defied the weather and been well rewarded by sights they would never forget. Everyone had done well on the descent, especially Mavis in that wretched cape of hers. And, by the way, would Bert be kind enough to let her have five copies of that photo he had taken.

Warm, dry, fed and watered, the group left the pub to rejoin the cars, all for one reason or another, well satisfied with the day's events. Walking alongside Bert with O.L. close by, Harry had a suggestion to make.

'That photo, Bert, what about blowing it up and framing it? It would look great hung on the wall in our meeting room in the pub. We could even add a motto – in Latin maybe, like a coat of arms, such as 'Dieu et Mon Droit' or 'Nemo Me Impune Lacessit.''

Bert grinned. He didn't know what the mottoes meant but he knew very well that Harry was taking the mickey. O.L., who did know what they meant, refused to rise to the bait. She would studiously ignore Harry Birch's infantile sense of humour.

SYD'S SNOWDON WALK

When Syd proposed taking Thurston Ramblers up Snowdon, O.L.'s eyes lit up. Snowdon had been on her wish list for years. Now here was Syd, the club's soft-spoken Welshman, born and bred in Betws-y-Coed, a strong walker who had climbed Snowdon many times, offering to make her wish come true.

In the club's room at the Rose and Crown, Syd had pinned up his 2½ inch map and was pointing out the possible ascents. O.L., an avid reader of climbing magazines and books, had already heard of most of the routes and kept nodding her head to show her familiarity with them. When Syd began to talk about Crib Gogh and the Snowdon Horseshoe, she couldn't restrain herself.

'That's it, Syd! That's the one we'll do.'

There followed a hushed silence. Syd had made it clear that Crib Gogh was a challenge even for experienced hill-walkers. The path was rocky, some scrambling was involved, way-finding in parts was not clear and, above all, there were scary sections and a knife-edge ridge with huge exposure. Harry was the first to protest.

'Hold your horses, Olive. You seem to forget we're ramblers not commandos. How many of us would want to risk life and limb on Crib Gogh? Count me out for a start.'

'Actually, Mr Birch, I never counted you in,' replied O.L. tartly. 'In fact, I'd be very much surprised if you could manage the Pyg route to Snowdon, let alone Crib Gogh. As for completing the Horseshoe over Y Lliwedd .....'

At this point, Gladys chipped in. She would like to know more about the Pyg route. She didn't have much of a head for heights and the mere thought of an exposed, knife-edge ridge sent shivers running down her spine. Would Syd be good enough to say more about the Pyg route? If it was easier than Crib Goch, she might just manage it.

Pointing out on his map the car-park at Pen-y-Pass, Syd continued, 'The Pyg route starts here at 359 metres on a tarmac path. After a gentle climb taking about 45 minutes, it reaches Bwlch y Moch at 569 metres. Here, the Crib Gogh path goes up steeply on the right but the Pyg continues westwards, climbing gradually for about two miles until it reaches a wall where the zigzags begin. There's now a steepish climb to the mountain railway at 998 metres which you follow up to the summit at 1085 metres. Nothing you couldn't cope with, Gladys. I think even Harry could do it in one of his good days – with a following wind.'

Syd's description of an easier option to Crib Gogh and his joke at Harry's expense lightened the mood. Penny pointed out that the cafeteria at the summit would be a great incentive, although she couldn't guarantee that Guinness would be on sale for Harry. Bert thought it would take more than Guinness to get Harry up Snowdon. O.L., still smarting from Harry's earlier reference to commandos, mustered a weak smile at this and offered to donate £10 to charity if she ever saw Harry on the top of

Snowdon. Harry smiled in return but said nothing.

O.L. was not going to forego Crib Gogh without a fight. Turning to Mike and Joe, the club's 'hard men,' she asked if they, at least, were up for it. When Mike said he had enjoyed doing it ten years ago and would enjoy doing it again, Joe nodded in agreement. O.L. then asked Syd if he had any objection to the three of them doing Crib Gogh while the main group did the Pyg track. They could all meet up in the cafeteria on the summit and go on to complete the horseshoe over Y Lliwedd.

Syd saw no objection. He had absolute confidence in the ability of Mike and Joe if rather less in O.L. She was, after all, some twenty years older than they. All the same, Syd felt that she made up in grim determination and stamina what she lacked in youth.

Now it was Penny's turn to seek reassurance. If not as accident-prone as her friend Gladys, Penny was not comfortable over rough ground and steep slopes. When she asked Syd how difficult the second leg of the horseshoe was, she was told about a tricky scree slope down from the summit followed by some scrambling up to Y Lliwedd followed by a descent along the ridge to the rough and rocky path leading down to Llyn Llydaw and ending with the Miners' Track back to Pen-y-Pass.

All of which did nothing to reassure her. Syd did his best to take the worried look off her face telling her it was all down to time. If she walked carefully at her own pace and took her time, all would be well. And the views from the ridge would more than compensate for a few aches and pains. Penny thanked him but still looked doubtful. As did Gladys.

Syd went on to talk about dates and times. He had chosen the last week in June before the school holidays; there would be fewer walkers on the mountain and less risk of finding the car park full at Pen-y-Pass. They would meet at 6 p.m. on the Friday, travel by car to his home town of Betwys-y-Coed and stay two nights at a hotel for B&B and evening meal, He'd already been in touch with the owner, an old friend of his, who was willing to give them a 20% discount. Syd paused to let the murmurs of approval die down. They would have breakfast at 7.15 on the Saturday, leave the hotel at 8 and get to the Pen-y-Pass car park for about 8.30.

To no-one's surprise, Harry couldn't see the point of such an early start. Getting up before 7 on a Saturday was just not natural. Anyone would think they were in the army. All this military precision! Would someone be blowing reveille on a bugle? Would there be a kit inspection after breakfast? Would they have to polish their boots? Would defaulters be confined to barracks?

Harry was enjoying himself. He liked an audience. Usually given only bit-parts in the town's Amateur Dramatic Society, here he was centre stage. With no director to tell him to tone it down, he had free rein to play to the gallery. There were smiles all round. This was what members of Thurston Ramblers expected of him. No-one took him too seriously. No-one, that is, except O.L.

'Really, Mr Birch,' she exclaimed, ' it's a pity you were never in the army. I've always thought it was a big mistake to abolish National Service. A bit of discipline would have done you good. Whingeing about an early start is so pathetic. In any case, I don't imagine for a moment that we'll have the pleasure of your company on Snowdon. It's not really your kind of walk, is it.'

'Now there, Olive, you could be wrong,' replied Harry coolly. 'I need a really outstanding photo for the camera club's annual competition and Snowdon could be just the place to find it. I'm not saying I'll make it to the top, mind you, but I think you can count on having the pleasure of my company for at least part of the way.'

To prevent hostilities escalating out of control, Syd intervened. He needed to know who was going, who was sharing twin rooms, who wanted singles and which drivers were taking which passengers. Would they discuss these matters over drinks and let him know before leaving. When the dust had settled, Syd had 14 names. They would travel in 4 cars and would need 6 twin rooms and 2 singles, O.L. as befitted her position as president, opting for one and Harry, saying he was a heavy snorer, the other.

O.L. was well pleased with the way things had turned out. Harry Birch had, as usual, tried to undermine her authority but she had told him a few home truths. More importantly, thanks to Mike and Joe, she would at last be able to tick off Crib Gogh and the Snowdon Horseshoe. It was not until the euphoria of the evening had worn off that she realised that Syd had not proposed a walk for the Sunday. She would have to bring it up at the next meeting. The opportunity of adding another prestigious walk to the Horseshoe was not to be missed. Her mouth watered at the prospect of scrambling up Tryfan or Carnedd Llewelyn.

At the next meeting, however, O.L.'s suggestion of

another long walk after the Horseshoe was not met with enthusiasm. Syd thought Tryfan would be too taxing: after the Horseshoe, they wouldn't feel like another big climb. A low-level walk from Betwys to Swallow Falls, for example, might be a better idea. To O.L., low-level was a euphemism for geriatric but she could hardly say so in public: she would have a quiet word with Mike and Joe later.

But even they had reservations. Mike wanted to wait and see how they felt on the Sunday morning and what the weather forecast said. With this, O.L. had to be content. At least she found it more acceptable than the suggestion of that wimp Harry Birch: the very idea of Thurston Ramblers strolling along a beach on Anglesey and paddling in the sea! What on earth would the man suggest next? Buckets and spades and kiss-me-quick hats, she wouldn't wonder.

On the evening of departure for Bewys-y-Coed, thirteen members of the group and three cars had assembled at the car park at 6 p.m. Ten minutes later, a red, two-seater, open-topped sports car screeched to a halt and Harry got out, greeted by a slow hand clap, led by Bert. Harry bowed in acknowledgement, smiling broadly. He humbly begged forgiveness for being late … rush-hour traffic … red lights against him … but O.L. cut him short.

'Yes, yes, Mr Birch, we've all had to cope with that. Now, if you don't mind, perhaps we can make a start: we've wasted enough time already.'

By the time they had all arrived at the hotel, located their rooms, washed and brushed up and found the dining room, most of the other guests had finished their meals and left. The manager looked none too pleased but raised a smile when Harry thrust a pint of Guinness into his hand. To avoid complications and speed things up, Syd had ordered a set meal for their arrival: tomato soup, fish, chips and peas followed by apple crumble and custard.

His choice met with general approval but Penny said she was allergic to fish so could she have ham salad, Mavis was on a diet so couldn't have chips or crumble, Bert fancied a hot curry and Harry preferred steak to fish. O.L. bristled at these requests: she had no patience with what she termed fussy eaters; people should eat what they were offered and be thankful.

The prompt arrival of the soup went some way to placate O.L. but it was a good fifteen minutes before the various main courses appeared. In the interval, she took the opportunity to have a few words.

'Your attention, please, ladies and gentlemen. May I remind everyone about tomorrow's early start: breakfast will be served at 07.15 and we leave at 8 … promptly.' With a meaningful glance at Harry, she added, 'Heavy traffic shouldn't be a problem getting from here to the car park outside so I expect everyone to be on time. I recommend an early night in view of tomorrow's exertions. Don't forget to fill your water bottles. I take it we have all brought our picnics.'

'Picnics!' shrieked Penny, 'I thought we were going to eat at the cafeteria. I've only got some Kendal Mint Cake and a Mars Bar.' O.L. looked pointedly at Penny's well-rounded figure.

'Well, I think you'll survive, Penny, but don't forget

we'll be out for about ten hours. What you need is a packet of nuts and raisins in your pocket to maintain your energy levels. Like that you won't have to stop walking to refuel. I've got a spare packet in my emergency rations so you'll be all right.'

Penny thanked her, adding sotto voce to Mavis that if O.L. thought nuts and raisins meant walking non-stop, she would do without them. Mavis, who also liked frequent pauses, offered her one of the bananas she'd brought.

Harry surprised everyone by being on time for breakfast. When his pal Bert led the applause, he bowed graciously As always, he was immaculately dressed. His brand new silver wind-proof trousers and sky blue reversible shirt drew cries of admiration from Mavis and Betty. Harry obliged them with a twirl. Then, by way of an encore, he produced, like a conjurer, the broad-rimmed Tyrolean hat complete with feather which he'd bought on Penny's recommendation two days ago. More applause and laughter mingled with yodelling from Joe and Mike. O.L. was not amused.

'Typical,' she muttered to Gladys, 'he's all show and no substance' whereupon Gladys, who had a foot in both camps, replied, 'That's as maybe, Olive, but you can't deny that he scrubs up well.'

Syd was pleased when they arrived at Pen-y-Pass car park at 08.30. The four cars had no trouble parking and the weather was warm with patches of blue sky among light cloud. O.L. was jubilant. The first to be booted and gaitered, she couldn't wait to get moving. Harry was in no such haste. Just when everyone was ready to go, he called for a group photo.

'Get someone to take it,' shouted Mavis, 'we can't have a group photo without you in that hat.'

When a lady just getting out of her car offered to take the photo, Harry spent some time deciding where exactly to stand, taking background and light into consideration.

'Over here everyone, please,' he called, 'Ladies in front, gentlemen behind, and take your sunglasses off, Betty, if you don't want to look as if you've been in a punch-up.'

When three shots had been taken, Harry pronounced himself satisfied and thanked the lady profusely. Even then, it was only after Joyce had decided she had better take advantage of the facilities, that they were able to move off, Syd and O.L. in the lead with Harry, Gladys and Penny bringing up the rear.

The first phase, a gentle ascent of 210 metres to Bwlch Moch – Pass of the Pigs, Syd informed them – presented no problem but when the steep outline of Crib Gogh came into view, Penny was horrified.

'We're not going up there, are we, Syd?' she gasped.

Syd told her not to worry, she was looking at Crib Gogh not Snowdon. Harry wasn't the only one to bring out his camera: O.L. had already envisaged the scene as the opening shot of the slide show she had offered to give to the Women's Institute in November.

At the pass, where the Crib Gogh path veered off to the right, O.L., Mike and Joe left the main party. Cries of 'good luck,' 'better you than me,' and 'watch where you're putting your feet,' followed them up the hill. Gladys hoped that Olive hadn't bitten off more than she could chew but Harry had no worries on that score, she was as tough as old boots and, in any case, the devil looked after his own.

It wasn't long before Snowdon itself came into sight. It looked formidable to Penny and Mavis but Syd said there was no hurry; they would be on the top in about three hours. Harry seemed more concerned with taking photos: he was particularly impressed by the jagged skyline of Lliwedd on the left with Llyn Llydaw below, a shot which would surely impress the Camera Club judges.

It was when he left the path to get the best view that he slipped. Gladys saw him fall and rushed forward to help.

'Nothing serious, Gladys, no bones broken,' he reassured her. 'Just turned my ankle. I think I'll have to go back when I've taken this photo.' Everyone was sympathetic.

'Rotten luck, Harry,' said Bert, 'I was looking forward to seeing O.L.'s face if you made it to the top. You haven't forgotten the £10 she said she'd give to charity if she saw you there, have you?' Harry shrugged his shoulders and said he hadn't forgotten and yes it was a great shame. Having assured Syd he didn't need any help, he wished them all good luck and limped off stoically back towards Pen-y-Pass.

Once out of sight, Harry abandoned his limp and quickened his pace. So far so good. He had given a convincing performance. Not for nothing his years in the Amateur Dramatic Society. The next stage in his plan should be easy: drive the five miles down to Llanberis, take the rack and pinion Mountain Railway to the summit and wait for the arrival of O.L. Anticipating her reaction to seeing him there made him laugh out loud, startling a sheep which scurried off into the bracken. He pictured a scenario where he would suddenly emerge from behind a rock, saying 'Mrs Jonstone, I presume.' He imagined her spluttering, lost for words, flabbergasted.

Harry had done his homework. Allowing an hour to walk back to his car, 15 minutes to get to Llanberis, a wait of perhaps 20 minutes for the train and about an hour to get to the top of Snowdon, he should arrive before both the main party and the splinter group of Mike, Syd and O.L. In order to give O.L. the impression that he had walked up with the others, he aimed to meet them at the top of the Pyg track and walk back up with them to the cafeteria.

At Llanberis station, he debated whether to buy a return ticket or a single. He had no intention of scrambling over Lliwedd to complete the Horseshoe but, if the weather held out, he wouldn't mind walking back down the Pyg track if any of the others, Gladys and Penny for example, were so minded. On the other hand, if the weather were to change, there was absolutely no point in getting cold and wet, shrouded in mist. Harry looked at the sky: there were fewer blue patches now and the clouds were thickening. As an insurance policy, he decided on a return ticket. It wasn't cheap at £25 but he thought it a price worth paying to outsmart O.L.

Mist was swirling round the summit when Harry got out of the train. Putting on his state-of-the-art yellow anorak, he looked in the cafeteria. As expected, neither group had yet made it. Resisting the temptation to have a coffee, he followed the railway line down to where the Pyg track came up. If the splinter group emerged first, he would keep out of sight and wait for Syd with the others.

With visibility down to thirty yards, Harry peered into the gloom for ten minutes before he recognised Syd and Bert with a straggle of walkers behind them. Bert was the first to recognise Harry.

'Well, blow me down,' he exclaimed, 'I thought you'd be in the pub at Pen y Gwrd nursing a swollen ankle. Oh I get it, you've come up in the train, haven't you!'

Surrounded by an audience hanging on his every word, Harry gave an edited version of his doings from the time of his fall. Some pain-killer plus an elastic ankle bandage from his first-aid kit had worked wonders on the way back to Pen-y-Pass. So much so that he had hit on the idea of taking the train up from Llanberis to join them for lunch at the cafeteria. The rest he'd had in the train up had helped his ankle to resume normal service and now he felt fine.

Bert, who knew Harry of old, wondered if his appearance might have anything to do with O.L.'s promise to give £10 to charity if she saw him at the summit.

'As a matter of fact, it did cross my mind, Bert.' replied Harry, poker-faced. 'How I got here is beside the point. I suggest we don't complicate things by mentioning my ankle sprain and my return to the car-park. Or that I came up in the train. If she thinks I came up with you, on foot, she'll be dumbfounded.'

Betty thought it unlikely that O.L. would believe that Harry had walked up but Harry retorted maybe not but she couldn't deny that here he was on Snowdon and that she'd lost her bet.

It was 12.35 when they got up to the cafeteria by which time the mist had lifted and given way to a sunny period. Syd found a place outside where they could all picnic and Harry concealed himself behind a rock so that he could make an entry when Mike, Joe and O.L. appeared.

They didn't have long to wait. Mike and Joe showed no signs of fatigue but O.L. was limping.

'What happened, Olive? Are you O.K.?' cried Gladys.

O.L. sank wearily onto a rock and began to explain. She had found Crib Gogh harder than expected. The arête was scary but she had made it with the encouragement of Mike and Joe. Then the mist came down and it started to rain. It was when they were descending the second pinnacle that she had slipped on the wet rock. It could have been worse, much worse if her rucksack hadn't cushioned her fall. But it was nothing really. Just slowed her down, that was all. Mike had insisted on carrying her bag. The main thing was that she had done Crib Gogh and would everyone stop fussing and let her have something to eat. Then, as an afterthought, she looked round the group and asked how far Mr Birch had walked up the Pyg track before he'd had enough.

Harry, who had overheard everything, chose this moment to reveal himself, playing the role of Stanley meeting Livingstone with great panache. O.L. nearly fell off the rock she was sitting on. When she had recovered from the shock, she forced a smile, saying, 'Well, well, wonders never cease. Harry Birch getting to the top of

Snowdon! Who would have thought it? You didn't come up on a donkey, did you?'

'No, I did not!' retorted Harry, 'and may I remind you of your promise to donate £10 to charity if you saw me on the top of Snowdon. In view of your near-death experience on Crib Gogh, I think it should go to the Mountain Rescue people, don't you?'

O.L. was nonplussed. She had completely forgotten what she'd said, months ago, in the heat of the moment.

'Did I really say that?' she asked Gladys, who nodded.'Very well,' she muttered, 'if that's what I said, I'll stick by it. It is, after all a very worthwhile charity.'

During the picnic, Harry was elated: he had triumphed once again over O.L. As they were going into the cafeteria for coffee, Betty and Mavis asked for a quiet word.

'Harry, you can't go through with this, it's not right,' murmured Betty. 'You knew perfectly well what she meant – you getting up Snowdon on your own two feet.'

'You've conned her, Harry,' added Mavis, 'she's sure to find out sooner or later that you took the train and she'll be very upset that the rest of us kept quiet'

In his heart of hearts, Harry knew they were right. He had involved the others in a conspiracy of silence, a burden which Betty and Mavis – two of his fan club – felt uncomfortable with. No doubt they were not alone. Maybe he should put the record straight. He had had his bit of fun. Perhaps he should be satisfied with that.

Over coffee, Syd raised the question of what next. Clearly, O.L. was in no fit state to tackle the second half of the horseshoe – even she had to admit that. Mike and Joe were concerned about the unstable weather: scrambling over wet rock and scree would be tricky if not dangerous.

With O.L. silent, there was a distinct lack of enthusiasm to complete the horseshoe whereupon Syd said that they could either return all the way on the Pyg track or branch off it, part way down, to take the Miners' Track.

'Frankly, Syd,' interrupted Mike, 'in my view, Olive would be unwise to attempt to walk down at all. It's three hours, either way and she would almost certainly aggravate the damage to her ankle.' Turning to O.L., he continued, 'You've only one sensible option, Olive, you'll have to take the train down,'

O.L. bridled at the thought of taking the train down: she would manage, her ankle wasn't all that painful and it was downhill all the way. Strange to tell, it took Harry, Harry of all people, to make her see reason. Cutting short her protests, he started his speech by saying how everyone, himself included, admired her stiff upper lip attitude in the present situation.

'Would you be kind enough, Olive' he went on, ' to accept a small gift from me as a token of my esteem?' With a flourish, he handed her the return half of his train ticket.

O.L. hadn't been able to believe her eyes an hour ago when Harry suddenly appeared out of the blue; now she couldn't believe her ears. Was this really Harry Birch announcing, in public, that he admired her? Her confusion was masked by the applause, led by Betty and Mavis. It was only when she looked more closely at Harry's gift, having recovered her composure, that she began to put two and two together.

'A return ticket!' she exclaimed. 'So you came up in the train. I might have known it. Trust you to play a trick like that!'

Harry held up his hands. 'Now Olive, don't be offended; it was just my little joke. To make amends, I'm offering you my seat in the train. Think of it as a peace offering. And you can forget about the donation to Mountain Rescue.'

More applause came from Betty and Mavis, allowing O.L. time to consider her reply. True, she had been outsmarted but it would be churlish to reject Harry's peace offering. She thanked him with as much grace as she could muster.

'What about you, Harry?' asked Gladys, 'you'll be taking the train down as well, won't you? Your ankle can't have recovered so quickly.'

Harry smiled. His ankle had made a recovery that was nothing short of miraculous. As for going down by train, he had given it a brief thought but now he felt some fresh air would do him good and he'd walk down. Besides, there would certainly be more photo opportunities which it would be a pity to miss. There was, of course, the problem of collecting his car and picking up Olive but he was sure someone would take him down to Llanberis.

O.L. pricked up her ears at the mention of Harry's ankle, not having been present when he apparently slipped and had to limp back to Pen-y-Pass. When Gladys enlightened her, underlining how stoical he'd been, she was most impressed. Perhaps she had underestimated him.

Added to that, he was now going to walk down when he could take the train! Sacrificing his seat to her!

When, three hours later, they got down to the cars, Mavis drove Harry to Llanberis where he picked up O.L. and returned to the hotel. Meeting the others in the bar, O.L. summed up the day. She herself was disappointed at not completing the horseshoe but delighted to have climbed Crib Gogh. In any case, getting to the top of Snowdon by any route was quite an achievement and everyone deserved congratulations. In particular, she would like to thank Mr Birch whose spirit and generosity she had much underestimated.

Basking in the glow of this unexpected praise from O.L., Harry called for drinks all round, content to have buried the hatchet – for the time being at least.

MAVIS'S TEESDALE WALK

'Have you heard, Harry? We've got a mademoiselle coming with us on Sunday!' This from Bert, breathlessly, as Harry arrived at the club room in the Rose and Crown. 'She's called Monique. Mavis is bringing her. They've been pen-pals for years. Wait till you've seen her photo!'

A bachelor gay, though certainly not a gay bachelor, Harry's penchant for young ladies was well known. As soon as Mavis came in, he wasted no time in finding out more. But it wouldn't do to appear too curious and risk offending her – she was, after all, his number one fan and always laughed at his jokes. After the customary peck on the cheek, he remarked casually that he'd heard she had a visitor. Pity she hadn't brought her to the meeting tonight.

Mavis gave him all the details. Her visitor was called Monique and came from Chamonix in the French Alps. They had been writing to each other since their schooldays and now Monique, like herself, was a Primary School teacher. She wasn't due to arrive until tomorrow. It would be the first time she had stayed with Mavis although Mavis had visited her last year. Would Harry care to see her photo? Harry saw at once why Bert had been so impressed. Monique was of medium height, slim, blue-eyed and blonde: there was an alluring smile on her pretty, sun-tanned face.

'Looks nice,' he commented, concealing with difficulty his admiration.

'I take it she'll be walking with us on Sunday? Speaks good English, does she?'

Mavis said Monique was looking forward to joining them on Sunday. Her English was quite good although she sometimes made funny mistakes.

Harry was relieved to hear that. He had never distinguished himself at French and just about the only words he remembered from a school exchange visit some thirty years ago were 'merde' and 'zut.' To make an impression, he would have to do better than that. Maybe he could get hold of a CD on conversational French: he'd have a word with Penny who worked in the library.

Before Mavis began to talk about the trip to Teesdale, she told all present about her visitor and tactfully asked the president if she could bring Monique. O.L. had no objection in principle to guests, always providing they were good walkers. No need to worry on that score, Mavis assured her. Living in the Alps, Monique was used to walking: she had done the Tour of Mont-Blanc two years ago. Visibly impressed by this, O.L. said Monique would be very welcome, adding after a pause, that it was a pity they weren't going to the Lakes on Sunday; Monique would have found it more inspiring than a nature walk in Teesdale.

Rather nettled, Mavis retorted that Monique was, in fact, very interested in nature, besides which, her walk was by no means a doddle. It was 12 miles long, there were a few quite steep climbs and some of the paths were rough. This was not good news for Harry who had fondly envisaged sauntering round a botanical garden.

'Any chance of liquid refreshment half way round,?' he inquired, 'We wouldn't want to get dehydrated, would we?'

Giving Mavis no chance to reply, O.L. suggested curtly that he take an extra bottle of water and could they now hear what Mavis had to tell them about the walk?

'It's an early start,' resumed Mavis. 'If we leave at 7, we should get to the starting point at Bowlees Visitor Centre, three miles west of Middleton-in-Teesdale, by about 9. You'll see that I've highlighted our route on the map. We walk down to the main road, cross the Tees at Wynch bridge and meet the Pennine Way just below Low Force.'

When O.L. realised they'd be walking on the Pennine Way, she pricked up her ears: she would read what Mr Wainwright had to say about it in his Pennine Way Companion when she got home.

'Low Force is the first of a series of waterfalls we shall meet,' continued Mavis. 'It's not so awe-inspiring as High Force but I think it's prettier with its rock formations and islands covered in marsh marigolds just below the falls. Whatever you do, don't forget your cameras: this walk is a photographer's dream.'

'What about having an exhibition when we get back, some time in December, maybe?' proposed Harry enthusiastically. He went on to suggest various categories such as flowers, birds, waterfalls and landscapes. They could make it into a competition for the best photo in each category. He could get one of his friends from the Camera Club to do the judging. Prizes could be awarded.

O.L. never took kindly to proposals from the rank and file, much less than from Harry Birch who was always trying to upstage her. Her instinctive reaction was to question his motives. With his sophisticated camera, lenses and filters, he would have a clear advantage over the 'point and shoot' brigade, of which she was one. His idea of inviting a friend to do the judging didn't appeal to her either. There could be a suspicion of collusion if Harry's photos were declared the best. All the same, she thought it wasn't a bad idea and regretted not having thought of it herself. Asserting her authority, she declared in measured tones, 'I do think it could make an interesting evening, Mr Birch, but it's a matter for the committee to decide. Incidentally, I don't see why we need an outsider as judge: we can decide on the winners ourselves by secret ballot. Now, I suggest we get back to the business in hand and let Mavis continue.'

Mavis picked up where she had left off. Further upstream, there were masses of juniper trees of all shapes and sizes: this was the place to make for if they fancied making gin. The berries took two or three years to turn purple and ripen: she didn't advise anyone to sample the green ones which were extremely bitter.

Next came High Force which they would hear long before they reached it: it was the biggest though not the longest waterfall in the country. There was a dramatic 70 foot vertical fall as the Tees plunged over an outcrop of the Great Whin Sill. She hoped the river would be in spate to see it at its best.

They would keep on the Pennine Way alongside the river for another mile when there was a good chance of sighting dippers, grey wagtails and possibly a kingfisher. They would then take a path to join the track coming from Holwick Scar to climb across open moorland to Cronkley Fell, part of the Upper Teesdale National Nature Reserve. Here, they would find seven enclosures erected to protect endangered species, notably the Spring Gentian. This was the emblem of the Reserve: the size of a daisy, it was like a five pointed star with brilliant blue petals. Another flower which would delight them was the Bird's Eye Primrose. It also flourished on limestone and looked like a small pink cowslip with a yellow eye in the centre.

Unable to suppress his admiration for the way Mavis was describing the walk, Harry once again interrupted.

'I wish I'd had a teacher like you, Mavis, when I was a lad. I'd have been top of the class!' Bert, who had been in Harry's class at primary school, thought that highly unlikely.

'Come off it, Harry,' he cried, 'you were always getting into trouble at school. You always had to sit in the naughty boy's seat in the front where the teachers could keep an eye on you.'

Harry protested that was only because he'd never had a teacher like Mavis: if he had, he'd have been teacher's pet for sure. When a voice from the back asked if he didn't mean teacher's pest, O.L. suppressed a smile and called for order. Would Mr Birch kindly be quiet. This was not the time to indulge in idle speculation. Perhaps he would allow Mavis to finish what she had to say.

'There's a steep downhill section from Cronkley Fell down to the river where we'll picnic opposite Falcon

Clints,' continued Mavis. 'Cauldron Snout, coming down from Cow Green Reservoir, can be seen from a point half a mile upstream: it might be worth the detour if the visibility is good. We now head downstream below the cliffs of Cronkley Scar where we may see buzzards and other birds of prey. Eventually we rejoin the Pennine Way where we left it earlier in the day. The last lap takes us back for another look at High Force and Low Force before we get back to the Visitor Centre.'

'Sounds great,' said Gladys, 'mustn't forget the binoculars. I imagine there'll be plenty of stops on the way.'

Mavis hesitated. She'd been on nature walks before and knew how keen botanists and bird-watchers could slow down the pace of a group.

'We'll certainly not be rushing, Gladys,' she replied, 'but it's a long walk and the terrain is rough at times so we can't afford to linger too much. I'm sure we would all like to get back to the Visitor Centre for tea before it closes at 5 o'clock.'

On the morning of the walk, 14 members of Thurston Ramblers had assembled at the car park promptly at 7 o'clock. For once, Harry was early. Penny guessed at once the reason: he wanted to be the first to greet Monique and try out the French he'd learned from the CD she'd found for him in the library. Immaculate as ever, he exuded bonhomie to all and sundry while keeping a sharp lookout for the arrival of Mavis and Monique.

Monique had hardly got out of the car when Harry, not waiting for Mavis to introduce him, rushed forward, bowed, seized her hand, kissed it and exclaimed, 'Enchanté, mademoiselle, de faire votre connaissance. Je vous souhaite la bienvenue chez nous. Je m'appelle Harry. A votre service, mademoiselle.'

Monique was taken aback by this unexpected display of gallantry but managed to thank him and congratulate him on his very good French. Then, turning to Mavis, she whispered, 'Monsieur est le président de l'association?'

At this point, O.L., who had been hovering behind Harry, squirming at his effusive language and unseemly behaviour, pushed forward and was introduced by Mavis as 'madame la présidente' O.L. contented herself with a brief 'bonjour' before going on, in English, to welcome Monique hoping she would enjoy today's walk in a beautiful part of England with Thurston Ramblers.

Monique thanked her, saying her English was not very good and adding:

'I am very much looking forward since a long time to walking in England with English ramblers.'

'British ramblers, if you please Monique, Syd's a Welshman and I'm a Scot,' cried Joe.

Monique begged their pardon and hoped she hadn't offended them but Bert told her not to worry, there was no difference really, they just had a funny accent.

The sun was shining when they arrived at Bowlees Visitor Centre just after 9 o'clock To the relief of everyone, especially Joyce, the toilets were open but Harry was dismayed to learn that there was no chance of coffee as the cafeteria didn't open until 10.30. Mavis and O.L. on the other hand, were pleased: both were both eager to be off.

Having crossed the bridge over the Tees, they joined the Pennine Way and headed upstream where Low Force brought forth cries of admiration. Mavis had said it was pretty but Gladys thought it beautiful. She spent some time discussing with Penny the best angle from which to take a photo. It wasn't just the white water cascading down through the rocky channels that appealed to her; it was also the river bed below dotted with rocks, small islands and flowers. In the end, she, like several others, took shots from below looking up, from the top looking down and from the middle looking across.

Mavis rounded up her flock with difficulty but she could only count twelve. Harry was conspicuous by his absence – as was Monique. When they eventually arrived, Harry said he'd been instructing their French visitor in the finer arts of photography and got rather carried away. Ignoring Bert's leer and O.L.'s snort, he went on to say he'd taken a brilliant photo of the falls with Monique in the foreground, sitting on a rock.

As they approached the juniper wood, Mavis asked Monique what she thought of Harry.

''Arry is a funny man: 'e makes me laugh,' was her verdict.

Mavis told her that Harry certainly had a sense of humour but he didn't make their president laugh. She thought he was a wimp and he thought she was a dragon. Mavis wished she'd used some other word than wimp: it took her several minutes to explain what it meant before Monique seemed to understand.

'You mean Arry is not the kind of man one would meet on the Tour du Mont-Blanc?' she enquired.

'Exactly!' said Mavis, 'unless he could find a mule to carry him round.'

The sound of rushing water increased to a thunderous roar as they drew nearer to High Force. Mavis proposed a combined coffee/photo break of ten minutes and the group dispersed, cameras at the ready. The river was not in spate as Mavis had hoped but the fall still made an impressive spectacle. Gladys, an accident waiting to happen, according to O.L., had to be restrained from clambering over rocks to get a good angle while Harry, unable this time to prise Monique away from the clutches of Mavis, had to content himself with Bert to initiate into the finer arts of photography.

Staying on the Pennine Way for another mile as it ran close to the river, kept the bird-watchers happy. Penny, the club's acknowledged ornithologist, was the first to spot the dipper bobbing up and down on a rock. Calling the group to a halt, she passed her binoculars to Monique who immediately recognised the bird as a 'cincle plongeur' and asked Harry if he could take a photo of it. Harry was only too willing to oblige and offered to supply her with a print if she could meet him at the Rose and Crown the following evening and would 8 o'clock be convenient. Monique was given no time to reply Just as he was adjusting his zoom lens, a piercing shriek came from O.L who was clutching her upper thigh.

'I've been stung,' she cried, 'I think it's a wasp.'

The dipper didn't wait for an encore and vanished upstream, leaving Harry deprived of what might have been a prize winning photo and, more importantly, of the pretext for a rendez-vous with Monique. This was a 'zut' and 'merde' moment if ever there was one but he managed to restrain himself in the presence of Monique. It was only when O.L. had retired discreetly behind a bush, closely followed by Gladys, to inspect the sting and apply an antidote, that Harry gave vent to his frustration, telling Bert that he wouldn't be surprised if O.L. hadn't faked the wasp sting just to thwart him.

'In that case,' replied Bert, not overly sympathetic, 'she's a pretty good actress. You should get her to join your Drama Club.'

Harry briefly pondered this possibility and then said that if they ever did 'The Taming of the Shrew' he would put her name forward.

Having regained her composure and showing a stoical indifference to the wasp sting, O.L. rejoined the group.

Harry was in a dilemma as they got nearer the path which would take them away from the Pennine Way on the climb up to Cronkley Fell. He had intended to give it a miss, potter about by the river, maybe have a nap and wait for the others on their way back. But so far, he hadn't been able to make much headway with Monique. If he were to leave the group now, he would have less time to make an impression. Finally, he resolved to stay with the group in spite of the climb ahead.

To the surprise of everyone except Bert, Harry strode on to join Mavis and Monique in the lead. Walking behind Harry was a novel experience for O.L

'Mr Birch is in remarkably good form today,' she muttered to Gladys, 'anyone would think there was a pub at the top of this hill.'

Gladys suggested it might have something to do with his recent visits to the gym but Bert thought it more likely that he wanted to practise his French.

In spite of being breathless as the path became steeper and stonier, Harry produced another of the phrases he had learned from Penny's tape.

'Ça va, Monique?' he enquired.

Monique replied in French that she was fine, the views over the valley were lovely, it was a beautiful walk and she was enjoying herself. As this reply had not figured on his tape, Harry was left stranded but he gathered from Monique's body language that all was well and he had the presence of mind to say 'bon.' Reverting to English, he repeated his invitation to the Rose and Crown the following evening. It was a pity O.L.'s shriek had frightened off the dipper but he would have plenty more photos to show her.

Monique asked Mavis if this would be all right by her whereupon Mavis thanked Harry and said they would both be delighted to see his photos. Bert, who had now overtaken them, said he too would like to join them if Harry had no objection. Forced to abandon his planned tête-à-tête with Monique, Harry hid his frustration with a less than enthusiastic 'O.K., the more the merrier.'

At the top of the fell, the path levelled out, its surface covered with what looked like coarse grains of sugar. This, explained Mavis, was the crystallised limestone which enabled plants such as the spring gentian to establish themselves. The enclosures were to protect them and other endangered species from the sheep.

In her haste to investigate, Gladys left the path, stumbled and fell headlong into a ditch. Picking herself up, she brushed aside expressions of concern, glared at the ditch as if it had no right to be there and hurried on to where Harry, on his knees, was taking a photo. The clump of gentian he'd spotted, fully open in the sun, brought forth cries of admiration. Further afield, Penny had found a mass of bird's eye primrose and Monique was enthusing over some yellow mountain pansies.

Mavis again had some difficulty rounding up her flock. Last to arrive was Joyce who had been obliged to go off at a tangent in search of a rock where she could discretely relieve herself.

The track down to the Tees where they were to picnic was steep and rutted. Mavis advised caution; walking sticks would be helpful. To O.L., a walking stick was only a short step away from a zimmer frame. She was prepared to admit that Gladys could find one helpful but for real walkers, a stick, in her opinion,was quite unnecessary. As far as she was aware, Mr Wainwright only resorted to a stick when his sight was failing. As for walking poles, they were ostentatious foreign imports more suitable for Arctic explorers probing for crevasses than walkers in Great Britain.

As they slowly picked their way down, the moorland silence was shattered by 'oohs,' 'ahs' and giggles. A pair of red grouse rose in protest, their rapid wing beats and strident 'go back' calls adding to the cries of the walkers. Penny pointed her camera at them as they glided away but wasn't sure she had caught them. Harry took it upon himself to keep an eye on Gladys, this act of chivalry not going unnoticed by the ladies. When they were safely down, Monique was heard to remark to Mavis,

''Arry ees a gentleman, ees 'e not?'

Harry's status as a gentleman needed no confirmation from Mavis when, at the picnic spot, he offered Monique his sit-mat. Basking in her approval, Harry now played his trump card. Delving into his bag, he produced two 25cl bottles of wine and two plastic cups. Clearing his throat, he turned to Monique and asked, in a very plausible French accent,

'Alors, mademoiselle, qu'est-ce que vous préférez, le rouge ou le blanc?'

Bert whistled in admiration and Penny clapped, but O.L. was wide-eyed with disbelief. Not at Harry's French, unexpected as that was, nor at his blatant flirting with Monique which she could have predicted. What upset O.L. was the wine. No-one in the history of Thurston Ramblers had ever brought wine to drink at a picnic during a walk. It just wasn't done. It was well known that alcohol led to dehydration, slowed down one's speed of reaction and affected balance. Typical of Harry Birch to ignore such things. The man was impossible. Unable to restrain herself, she blurted out,

'I must say, Mr Birch, that I strongly disapprove of wine-drinking in the middle of a walk. The reasons to most of us are obvious. If you have an accident on the way back, don't expect any help from me or the rest of us.'

O.L.'s outburst was followed by an embarrassed silence. In order to prevent the dispute from escalating, Gladys, ever the peacemaker, didn't give Harry the chance to reply, saying that she was sure they all agreed in principle with the president but that perhaps such a small bottle could do Mr Birch no harm, nor, for that matter their French visitor who was no doubt accustomed to drinking wine. This view seemed to meet with general approval but O.L. was not convinced.

To everyone's surprise, it was Monique who succeeded in restoring harmony.

'It ees very kind of 'Arry to bring wine for me but, in fact, I am not used to drinking wine on walks. Maybe at Christmas and jours de fête but never on walks. Ça me couperait les jambes, 'ow you say that in English, Mavis ?'

Mavis said the literal meaning was 'it would cut off my legs' but she would just say 'it would go to my legs.'

'There you are,' cried O.L. triumphantly, 'that's exactly what I meant. What good is a walker without legs? Nothing but a liability!'

'You're back in the naughty boy's chair, Harry,' cried Bert defusing what might have led to open confrontation. 'I remember when Miss Jones called you a liability for stuffing inkwells with blotting paper. We had a good laugh about that.'

Harry swallowed the retort he was going to make to O.L. and grinned.

'If you find me legless this afternoon, Bert, after one glass of wine, you can laugh your socks off. I might even offer you the other bottle ... if it won't make you legless, that is.'

When Bert readily accepted, Harry passed him the bottle and cup destined for Monique, not forgetting to cry 'santé,' another word he'd learned from the tape, under the baleful glare of O.L.

After the picnic, Joe, Mike and O.L. decided to walk upstream to get a view of Cauldron Snout giving Harry the chance to further his acquaintance with Monique. It surprised him that she didn't drink wine. He thought everyone in France drank wine and ate frogs' legs and snails.

'Not so,' replied Monique, 'I personally 'ate frogs and snails.'

'You've eaten frogs and snails?' he enquired, puzzled.

'Yes,' she replied, 'but only once. I 'ated them.' When the penny dropped, Harry laughed and had her repeating 'hate' and 'hated' a dozen times. For good measure, he added 'have,' 'hedge' and 'Harry.' In return, she made him say 'tu as bu un bon vin blanc,' a phrase which caused him great difficulty and brought peels of laughter from Monique. When Bert came over to find out what was so funny, Harry got him to say the phrase and was pleased to hear Bert's accent made Monique laugh even louder.

With all the group reassembled, Mavis announced that they would now follow the river downstream for about two miles, passing below the cliffs of Cronkley Scar, to rejoin the Pennine Way. There was a good chance of seeing buzzards, kestrels or even a peregrine but the path could be wet and slippery in places and they would have to watch where they were putting their feet.

'Especially you two,' added Penny, looking at Harry and Bert who promptly began to totter about as if legless, their performance amusing everyone except O.L.

To demonstrate how sure-footed they were, they then set off at a brisk pace ahead of Mavis, negotiating the slippery stretches with nothing worse than the occasional slither and reaching the Pennine Way a good three minutes before the pack. Gladys's rather tactless remark to O.L.

that she had never seen Harry walk so well and could the wine have anything to do with it, met with a snort.

Mavis looked at her watch. It was now 2.30. In her estimation, she told the group, it would take about two hours to get back to the Visitor Centre so they would have half an hour for refreshments and a look round before it closed at 5. Mavis had allowed for delays at High Force and Low Force when more photos would doubtless be taken but she had not allowed for the sheep with its horns entangled in the mesh of a wire fence.

First to the rescue was Harry, seeing an opportunity to further improve his status in the eyes of Monique. Unfortunately, as he was trying to release it, the panic-stricken animal reared up and kicked him on the leg, leaving Harry to beat a hasty and painful retreat. Joe, a police sergeant who had rescued cats from trees, terriers from rabbit holes and a pony stuck in a bog, now took charge.

To calm the sheep down, they needed to put something over its head, something like a baseball cap such as Harry was wearing. Harry, nursing his leg and beyond caring about the fate of his cap, duly obliged. After a struggle lasting several minutes, Joe, helped by Mike, managed to free the sheep which, still blindfolded, careered into a juniper bush and thrashed about until it had succeeded in getting rid of Harry's cap. When Joe retrieved it, scratched and dripping with saliva, Harry offered it to Bert who declined without thanks and rather rudely.

Harry received much sympathy from Gladys, Mavis and Monique who carefully inspected his calf but could find nothing more than a small bruise. The limp he developed grew less marked as their sympathy waned but nevertheless aroused the scorn of O.L. who had borne her wasp sting with stoic indifference and dismissed Harry's antics as malingering. Bert told him in no uncertain words to get a move on or they would miss their tea but Harry's brisk walk along the river, coupled with his close encounter with the sheep, had taken its toll and he almost fell. Bert told him that O.L. would have him on a charge of walking without due care and attention if he didn't buck up. If he fell, she would certainly gloat and put it down to the wine he'd drunk.

Spurred on, Harry straightened up and increased his pace. Rejecting the chance to take more photos and only pausing occasionally to mop his brow, he was among the first to arrive at the Visitor Centre where he insisted on buying tea and scones for Mavis and Monique.

Mavis was pleased that her walk had gone well. The weather had been perfect for walking, they had seen a good number of flowers and birds and taken some interesting photos. Everyone was in high spirits.

Monique declared that she would always have a good souvenir of her first walk with British ramblers. When Mavis suggested she meant memory rather than souvenir, Bert said he didn't see why Monique couldn't have both a good memory and a good souvenir: what he had in mind was Harry's baseball cap. Rising to the occasion to take centre stage, Harry presented his battered cap to Monique who gracefully accepted it, planting kisses on both his cheeks. At which, Penny led the applause and even O.L managed a smile.

GLADYS'S ISLE OF MAN WALK

Gladys had done her homework. It was just as well as her proposed walk on the Isle of Man, programmed for the first Saturday in September, provoked animated discussion in the club's meeting room at the Rose and Crown.

'I realise it's three months away,' said Gladys, 'but I need to know how many will be going to get the flights booked from Manchester.'

Harry maintained that flying from Blackpool would be more convenient. Penny said it made no difference to her, Manchester or Blackpool, as she was allergic to flying whereupon Bert suggested sailing from Heysham. O.L. wanted to know if a day trip would allow them enough time to do Gladys's walk. Joe nodded and proposed spending an extra day on the island to justify the cost of getting there.

Unfazed by this barrage of questions, Gladys said she was sorry about Penny being unable to fly but sailing from Heysham wouldn't give them enough time on the island. Flying was the only option. She conceded that flying from Blackpool was marginally more convenient than from Manchester but pointed out that planes on the Blackpool to Isle of Man route had only about nineteen seats which could make booking difficult for a group. If they flew from Manchester, they could be on the island by 09.10 and back in Manchester at 21.00. so they would have ample time for her leisurely walk.

Mention of a leisurely walk was greeted by a beaming smile from Harry. Predictably, O.L. was less enthusiastic: would Gladys kindly explain what she meant by a leisurely walk. She sincerely hoped they weren't going all that way for a stroll along the beach!

'Nothing wrong with a stroll along the beach,' retorted Harry. 'All that pure sea air to detox your lungs, a breeze rippling through your hair, soft sand under your feet, gulls wheeling round … and an ice-cream cornet to lick! My idea of paradise'

'You've forgotten to mention your bucket and spade,' snorted O.L., 'and the flags for your sand castle.'

To prevent hostilities escalating, Gladys quickly began to talk about her walk. It wasn't long – about 10 miles – and it would take roughly 5 hours, not counting stops. The starting point was Port St Mary at the south-west tip of the island. They would make their way, mostly on the cliffs lining the coast, to Port Erin and then climb up to Bradda Hill before returning to Port Erin for the short steam railway trip back to Port St Mary.

'What about places of refreshment?' asked Harry to nobody's surprise.

Gladys told him not to worry on that score. Half way round, at the Calf of Man, there was a Visitor Centre which provided meals … and ice-cream. Then, at Port Erin, there were several pubs, cafés … and ice-cream parlours.

'So what made you choose this particular walk, Gladys,' asked Mavis. 'I believe there are plenty of good walks on the Isle of Man, some quite hilly.'

'There certainly are,' replied Gladys, 'but this is my favourite. It's full of variety, twists and turns and ups and downs without being too hard on the knees. There are two interesting fishing ports we'll have time to look round and there's every chance of seeing seals at the Calf of Man. What makes it particularly attractive in early September is the profusion of yellow gorse and purple heather in full bloom.'

'I suppose you did consider climbing Snaefell, Gladys,' asked O.L. 'It would be very satisfying to stand on the highest point of the island. It's only 621 metres and the views all round must be superb. I think it's well within the scope of most of our members … if not all. Come to think of it, there's a café at the top. The prospect of an ice-cream cornet might even encourage Mr Birch to make the effort.'

Stung by this gibe, Harry retaliated. Referring obliquely to O.L.'s descent from Snowdon on the mountain railway, he said that the electric railway up Snaefell might be reassuring, encouraging even, to any of their members who were incapable of coming down on foot.

Gladys sensed that all present were enjoying yet another verbal spat between O.L. and Harry in his role of agent provocateur but she thought it had gone far enough.

'Coming back to your question, Olive, yes I did consider climbing Snaefell but not for long. It's mostly a dull trudge over featureless moor: I didn't think it worth the effort. Besides, the summit is so often covered by cloud, we'd be lucky to get any views at all. Anyway, you'll still have a chance to stretch your legs, Olive. To get to the top of Bradda Hill from Port Erin, there's a steady climb of about 220 metres.'

When Harry pulled a face at this, his pal Bert, trying in vain not to grin, told him there was a lovely sandy beach at Port Erin. If he didn't fancy the climb, he could take a stroll along the beach, buy a cornet and build a sand castle. He'd be in Paradise!

O.L. found this joke at Harry's expense highly amusing. Harry less so but he knew Bert well enough not to take offence. They often indulged in banter like this. When the laughter had subsided, Mike, always a stickler for detail, wanted to know how far Port St Mary was from Ronaldsway airport and would they have to hire transport to get there and back.

'It's only six miles so I'm suggesting we go by bus,' Gladys told him. 'It takes half an hour. I reckon we could be starting the walk about 10.15. and be back in Port St Mary about 17.30. That would give us a good hour to have a meal and get back to the airport by 19.15 for the 20.10 flight to Manchester. Now will everybody interested please sign up before you leave. I estimate the flight will cost £65 which I'd like to have either tonight or by the weekend.'

'One more question, Gladys, if you please,' called out Mike. 'We'd have to be at Manchester airport pretty early, wouldn't we? How do we get there?'

'Good question, Mike,' replied Gladys, 'We'd have to be at the airport for 07.30. There's no convenient train so we'd have to go by car, leaving at 06.30. O.K. Harry?

'Can't say I'm delighted, Gladys,' replied Harry. 'Not at my best at that time of day. But never fear, I'll make a special effort … just for you … and your leisurely walk. Mind you, that hill you mentioned is a bit of a turn-off. I might just follow my good friend Bert's suggestion and have a quiet stroll along the beach. Thinking of him puffing and panting up that that hill will make my ice-cream taste all the better.'

Gladys had given them all plenty to think about as they gathered in small groups to discus her proposals. Syd was concerned about the cost: it would be an expensive day trip and he wondered if he could afford it. What bothered Joyce was the early start and the late return: it would be a very long day. Joe brought up again the possibility of spending a night on the island: this would make Saturday less tiring and they could do another walk on Sunday. When several heads nodded in agreement, Mike put the question again to Gladys.

'I did think about a weekend, Mike, but there are snags. First it would add another £40 plus to the cost. Then there would be the problem of finding a B&B with enough rooms available. If we did another walk on the Sunday, being without cars, we'd almost certainly need to hire a bus to get to the starting point, collect us at the end, take us back to the B&B to collect our luggage and then to the airport. In my opinion, it would be much less complicated to make it a day trip.'

Mike looked unconvinced. As did Joe and O.L. Gladys was beginning to wish she'd chosen to lead a walk nearer home when Bert, to everyone's surprise, came up with a compromise.

'I'll lead a walk on the Sunday, if you like, Gladys, for anyone who wants to stay an extra day. We could pick up the coastal path where we left it at Fishwick Bay the day before and follow it up to Peel. I did it three years ago with my brother. He has a B&B in Port St Mary and I dare say he could find room for five or six of us.'

When Bert went on to say that it was quite a tough walk with two stiff climbs over rough moorland, O.L.'s eyes sparkled. This would compensate for the leisurely walk proposed by Gladys. It would also sort out the sheep from the goats. Harry Birch, for one, wouldn't be holding them back.

'Sounds great but would there be a problem with transport?' asked Mike.

'Not to get to the start,' replied Bert. 'My brother could get us to Fishwick Bay, no problem, but we'd have to check on the bus times back from Peel to the airport. If they're not convenient, we'd have to get a taxi.'

'Right, that's settled then,' cried O.L. briskly. 'Can we have a show of hands? I know you're interested, Mike and Joe, as much as I am. There's Bert, of course. You up for it too, Mavis? Good show. That makes five of us.'

None too pleased, Gladys shrugged her shoulders. More complications. So how many members preferred to return on the Saturday? Eight? Very well, she would leave the arrangements for Sunday to Bert and book the flights on line for both groups. They could decide later about who would drive who to Manchester airport.

As they were leaving the pub, Harry commiserated with Gladys. 'You might have guessed O.L. would put her spoke in. She doesn't improve with age, does she?'

Gladys, tolerant to a degree, laughed. 'Come to that, Harry, neither do you. You never miss a chance of putting her down, do you? But you know, Olive and I go back a long way. We understand each other. She means well and you have to admit she keeps us on our toes.'

'On our toes?' retorted Harry, 'on our knees, more like it, if I didn't put a brake on some of her sadistic ideas.'

On the day of departure, everything went according to plan. Bert had persuaded Penny to overcome her fear of flying so they now numbered 14. The plane was on time at Ronaldsway and they didn't have long to wait for a bus to Port St Mary.

On arrival, Harry suggested a coffee would freshen them up after their journey; maybe Bert's brother would oblige. Bert said his brother would not be overly delighted to see 14 people on his doorstep at that time of morning whereupon Mavis told Harry to try deep breathing: he would find a few lungfuls of sea air more invigorating than coffee. Gladys agreed and gathered the group together: there would be time when they got back to explore the town and port. They would start by walking along the sea-front to join the coastal path, the Raad ny Foillan, 'The Road of the Gulls,' which ran round the island for 95 miles.

'Before we make a start, Gladys,' interrupted Joyce, 'do you think we could find some toilets?'

By the time Joyce, and at least half a dozen others, had found relief, O.L. was champing at the bit and even Gladys was getting impatient. Harry, on the other hand, although deprived of his coffee, was happily taking photos of the yachts in the port. Conditions were perfect. The sun had appeared, the sky was clear, there was hardly a ripple on the grey-blue sea and gulls were swooping over the rocks below. Harry was in no haste to start moving.

For a coastal path, the Road of the Gulls out of Port St Mary was somewhat disappointing. Heading inland alongside a golf course, it went through a housing estate, joined a sunken lane and up a hill lined by high hedges.

'Where's the sea, Gladys?' cried Harry, 'we've not missed the path, have we?'

'No we haven't,' called back Gladys. 'you'll soon see the sea, don't worry.'

A few minutes later, the tarmac became a cart-track and Harry was reassured as the sea came back into view. Further along, a signpost marked The Chasms required explanation and Gladys called a halt. The headland they were approaching was criss-crossed by cliffs which had been split open by earth movement to reveal deep clefts, like crevasses in glacier. There were paths running along the rims but her advice was to resist the temptation to peer into the murky depths. Anyone not too sure-footed, like herself, could climb up an adjacent field and view the chasms safely from above.

To O.L., this advice was obviously intended for the chicken-hearted. When Gladys led the way up the field, she strode ahead, Mike and Joe, recalling her fall on Crib Goch, following close behind. Harry hesitated. He was tempted by the possibility of taking a prize-winning photo but decided in the end that discretion was the better part of valour. In the event, he need not have worried. When O.L. rejoined the group, she announced that the paths round the chasms presented no problem: you just had to be careful where you were putting your feet. It was certainly worth the detour, she added, making sure Harry was within earshot. She had taken some very interesting close-ups of ferns and flowers which she would show at their next meeting.

Strolling along at the back of the group, Penny was chatting with Mavis.

'I'm so pleased Bert encouraged me to fly; I wouldn't have missed coming here for anything. This grassy path is like a carpet. It makes me want to take my boots off and walk bare-foot.'

'What I like is not having to watch where my feet are going,' said Mavis. 'It's great to be able to look round and admire the view. This huge expanse of purple heather and yellow dwarf gorse is glorious and look, there's a linnet on that bush.'

A steep descent to a stream caused Gladys to wobble but she managed to stay upright with the help of her stick. After regaining the height lost, they now had a clear view of the Calf of Man and Gladys called for a pause. If they made themselves comfortable in the heather, she would have a word about it.

'You won't go on too long, will you, Gladys?' called Harry. 'I'm ravenous and I've a thirst like a dredger. We can't be far from the Visitor Centre café now, can we?'

O.L. wasn't the only one to think Harry out of order saying this. Betty, not known for beating about the bush, told him bluntly to shut up and listen to what Gladys had to tell them. Taken aback by this rebuke, Harry muttered an apology; he hadn't meant to give offence.

Unperturbed, Gladys went on. 'The Calf of Man that you see over there is a bird sanctuary, one of the most important in the British Isles. It's uninhabited but there are two wardens during the summer months and some self-catering cottages. I spent a weekend in one of them ten years ago. Magic! There were Manx Shearwaters, Guillemots, Razorbills, Shags and Cormorants. You'd love it, Penny. Then there's a colony of seals – with any luck we should see some today – and occasional sightings of basking sharks, whales and dolphins.'

'We'll get to the Visitor Centre in about twenty minutes. We're in good time so we don't need leave until 2 o'clock. That will give us plenty of time for a leisurely lunch and a good look round. O.K.? We don't need to stick together when we get there; just remember to be back at the centre for 2 p.m.'

There must have been a score of people, mostly with binoculars, dotted along the shore-line opposite the Calf of Man.

'Almost certainly watching seals,' said Gladys, 'or even a shark.'

Harry's first priority was the café and Bert didn't need to be asked twice to join him. The others, led by Penny and Mavis headed down to the shore at a brisk pace. Their squeals of delight on seeing three seals bobbing about near the shore brought muffled cries of 'shush, you'll scare them' from people near by but Gladys thought this unlikely.

'These seals are used to being watched: they're as curious about humans as we are about them. Look, there are more basking on the rocks on the island.'

After ten minutes seal watching, the group walked up to the Visitor Centre to find Harry and Bert sitting at an outside table deep in conversation with two young ladies, obviously walkers.

'Meet Liz and Sue from Australia' called out Harry. 'They're students, bumming their way round the world. Working in a hotel in Port Erin just now. They've just walked down from there this morning. Seen two sharks on the way.'

Mavis pricked up her ears at this but Liz told her not to get too excited, the dorsal fins were all they could see above the water. They intended to explore the island on their next free day, seeing the sea birds and getting close to the seals. When Mavis told them there were three seals near the shore, the girls went off to see them, leaving Harry and Bert rather disgruntled to continue their lunch in the less exotic and less glamorous company of Syd and Betty.

O.L. took a dim view of eating in cafés when on a walk It didn't seem right somehow. She preferred to be self-sufficient. A real walker's picnic was a cheese sandwich, an apple and a bottle of water, made up beforehand. Ideally, eaten on a remote hillside, far from the madding crowd. Now, surrounded by noisy, over-dressed tourists, some having arrived by car, others by coach, she wondered why on earth Gladys had proposed lunch there. Quickly buying a sandwich, she left to look for a quiet spot outside.

The others, taking Gladys at her word, had a leisurely lunch and then wandered off in twos and threes, Mike and Joe to a geological exhibition, Mavis and Penny to the bird observatory, Harry and Bert to view the seals and Joyce to join the queue outside the ladies' toilet.

Oddly enough, the one person missing outside the Centre at 2 p.m. was O.L. Gladys was worried: she had never, ever, known Olive to be late for anything. When Harry said maybe she'd been kidnapped, Gladys told him sharply that it was no laughing matter. Something serious must have happened: they must spread out and look for her. By a quirk of fate, it was Harry who spotted her, fast asleep behind a rock. Red-faced, either by embarrassment or sunburn, O.L. made profuse apologies for causing delay and consternation in the ranks. Then, in the next breath, she said they must make up for lost time and set off at a cracking pace ahead of Gladys.

'Hold your horses, Olive,' shouted Harry, 'we haven't all had a siesta.'

Starting at sea-level, the path was becoming stonier as it climbed back on to the cliffs and there were rock outcrops to be negotiated. When O.L., Mike and Joe reached the top, they looked back to see Gladys and Harry bringing up the rear half a mile away.

'Not quite the leisurely walk you promised us, Gladys,' gasped Harry when they rejoined the group sprawled out in the heather.

'Put it down to memory loss.' Gladys replied, smiling. 'Ten years ago, I climbed up here in half the time. Funny how hills get steeper the older you get.'

Penny, whose dieting regime had not so far been a resounding success, was perspiring more than most. Mopping her brow and stemming the flow of drops trickling down her nose, she nevertheless declared that she wasn't complaining; quite the reverse.

'It's well worth a few drops of sweat to get grand

views like this, Gladys. Those swathes of purple heather and golden gorse set against the blue sea with those great cliffs in the background would have had Monet in raptures.

Grassy slopes took them down to Port Erin Bay. On the other side was Bradda Head, their next destination, topped by a substantial tower visible for miles around. Beyond that, Gladys told them, their path led up to Bradda Hill, at 221 metres, the highest point of the day's walk.

'I imagine there are superb views from the summit,' exclaimed O.L. with a glint in her eye. 'I can't wait to get up there. I hope we won't be wasting time in Port Erin.'

Harry promptly objected to the word 'wasted.' He, and he was sure he wasn't the only one, was looking forward to a leisurely stroll along the beach ... after calling at the ice-cream parlour Bert had recommended ... and maybe a congenial beer garden.

O.L. studiously ignored this expected reaction from Harry and strode on along the promenade, unaware that Bert had located his ice-cream parlour. Looking none too pleased, she retraced her steps to find everyone licking cornets which they said were delicious. Harry's offer to have one on him was curtly rejected.

Crossing the beach, Harry felt strangely invigorated. To everyone's surprise and O.L.'s scepticism, he stayed with them as they made their way through the delightful Bradda Glen to join the Coronation Path leading up to the tower. O.L.'s scepticism was not misplaced. As the path steepened, Harry's steps became slower and more laboured.

'Not used to all this sun,' he called out to Gladys. 'I'm dehydrated. Have to go back. Don't want to hold you up. See you at the station in about an hour.'

Up at the tower, O.L. learned of Harry's defection.

'Harry Birch dehydrated! That's a good one. He always feels dehydrated when he gets near a pub. I don't believe he ever intended coming up here in the first place.'

Gladys cut short further speculation about Harry by announcing that the tower beside them was erected by public subscription for a local benefactor, William Milner, who among other things, had the breakwater built at Port Erin.

'From here up to Bradda Hill,' she continued, 'we're on a narrow, stony path on the cliff top so watch how you go. To tell the truth, I'm not looking forward to it much myself.'

Mike and Joe exchanged glances. Sure-footed, Gladys was not. They would shepherd her along the path. It wouldn't do to have their leader come to grief.

Gladys stumbled once or twice but managed to stay upright along the cliff edge to everyone's relief. After a lengthy climb, O.L. was the first to set foot on the summit where the long, panoramic views did not disappoint her. Pre-empting Gladys, she pointed out the coast of Scotland to the north and the mountains of Ireland to the west while Bert identified local landmarks including Snaefell, 20 miles away.

On the steep descent towards Fishwick Bay through tall bracken and heather, Gladys wobbled more than she had done on the cliff edge. Twice she lost her balance and ended up on her bottom. Penny fared little better. On one especially steep section, she disappeared completely into the bracken and had to be hauled out by Mike and Joe.

'Good thing you're well padded, Penny,' cried Bert when she emerged looking none the worse. 'You certainly gave that sheep a fright.'

'Cheeky monkey,' retorted Penny. 'I'll give you a fright when I get on my feet,'

Down on firmer ground, Gladys consulted her watch. Allowing 40 minutes to get back to Port Erin, they would be in good time to catch the steam train back to Port St Mary and find somewhere to eat.

'I've a little surprise for you there,' piped up Bert, 'We won't have far to look for somewhere to eat. I had a word with my brother Bill a few days ago and he said we could eat at his place. He asked if fish, chips and mushy peas would suit us. He could order them from the chippy up the road and he would provide tea and apple crumble. Yes, Penny, you don't need remind me; I know you're allergic to fish. When you finally made up your mind to join us, I told Bill you couldn't eat fish and were on a diet so he said his wife would make you a salad. O.K?'

Penny told Bert that would be fine and she would forgive him his earlier fall from grace. Gladys thanked him for his initiative: it would save a lot of time and hassle and give them time to look round Port St Mary. Bert mustn't forget to ask his brother how much they owed him.

A mixture of country lanes, tracks and paths brought them to Port Erin golf course, through the town and to the station. Harry greeted them effusively, planted a kiss on Gladys's cheek, asked Mavis if her legs were aching, did Betty have any blisters, would Penny like some suncream and had Olive enjoyed the views.

85

'I see you've recovered from your dehydration, Harry,' remarked Bert. 'Find a congenial beer-garden, did you?

'As a matter of fact I did, Bert.' replied Harry. 'And would you believe, those two Australian girls turned up! It happened to be the hotel where they were working. Pity you weren't there. We missed you.'

'I'll bet you did! Like we missed you going up Bradda Hill,' retorted Bert.

The little train took only five minutes to get to Port St Mary station but it was well outside the town. When they finally reached Bill's B & B., there were sighs of relief as they found chairs and removed boots. By the time everyone had washed and brushed up, the fish and chips were on the table and they weren't allowed to get cold.

After the meal, O.L. got to her feet and made a little speech.

'I think it only appropriate that I, on behalf of you all, express thanks to Gladys for introducing us to the Isle of Man and to congratulate her on her choice of such a beautiful walk. I only hope the walk which five of us will be doing tomorrow proves to be as pleasant. I gather from Bert it's rather more strenuous but I'm sure we'll cope. Organising a walk, especially a walk like today's, involving cars, flights, buses and a train, takes a lot of time and patience and I'm sure you would all like to show Gladys how much her efforts have been appreciated.' When the applause had subsided, Harry, not to be outdone, stood up.

'May I crave your indulgence, ladies and gentlemen, not excluding Bert, to add my two pennyworth to the words of our respected president. We do not always see eye to eye, Olive and myself – you may have noticed – but on this occasion at least, I heartily endorse her every word. Gladys is – and I'm sure she won't mind my saying this – no spring chicken. But I ask you, how many ladies do you know of 70 years plus – I won't say plus what – who still have a spring in their step and a sparkle in their eye? She may be a tad unsteady at times on rough paths but whenever she falls down, she always gets up smiling. She may be a little slow going uphill … thank you Bert, I know she's not the only one … but she always gets there in the end. Gladys, you're a star. Long may you continue to twinkle.'

Harry's histrionics which produced ripples of laughter and more applause, left Gladys rather embarrassed. She thanked Olive and Bert for their kind, if flattering remarks and then suggested they all have a stroll down to the harbour after settling up with Bill: they had almost an hour before their bus left for the airport.

Walking along the sea-front with Mavis, Harry laughingly said they should keep an eye on O.L. some distance ahead in case she fell asleep on a bench.

'Don't you dare remind her about that, Harry Birch, she'd never forgive you,' cried Mavis. 'It's been a great day. Don't go and spoil it.'

Harry promised not to but he couldn't vouch for the future.

THE PRESIDENT'S WALK

'Well, Harry,' said Bert as they were sitting in the snug of the Rose and Crown, 'what do you think she's got lined up for us this time?'

'Something crazy, for sure,' Harry muttered. 'Last year it was that 10 hour slog over the Three Peaks in pouring rain; the year before it was a night walk on the Pennine Way over Kinder Scout. I shudder to think what she's dredged up this year.'

Bert told him not to worry. Harry hadn't gone on any of O.L.'s walks before and Bert would be very surprised if he would be going on this one, wherever it was.

Upstairs in the room allocated to Thurston Ramblers, Harry exchanged pleasantries with Mavis and Gladys before the meeting began. When O.L. got to her feet, she didn't need to wait for the chatter to subside. She had so far given no clues about her walk and everyone was eager to hear what she had in mind.

'Ladies and Gentlemen,' she began, 'I am going to start by whetting your appetite for my walk in 10 days' time. As you all know, I have never made a secret of my profound admiration for Mr Wainwright. In Book 4 of his masterly Pictorial Guide to the Lakeland Fells, I came upon a passage which I found particularly inspiring. I'm sure you would like me to read it to you.'

O.L. paused and looked round to gauge the reaction

to this suggestion. There were a few nods, a few smiles and several looks of apprehension, among them Harry's.

'In his chapter on Scafell Pike,' she continued, 'Mr Wainwright says: 'Once in a while, every keen fell walker should have a pre-arranged night out amongst the mountains. Time drags and the hours of darkness can be bitterly cold but to be on the tops at dawn is a wonderful experience and much more than recompense for the temporary discomfort. Hollow Stones is an excellent place for a bivouac with a wide choice of overhanging boulders for shelter, many of which have been walled-up and made draught-proof by previous occupants. Watch the rising sun flush Scafell Crag and change a black silhouette into a rosy-pink castle.'

O.L. paused again to allow the implications of her reading to sink in. This time, there were fewer smiles and more looks of apprehension. Harry was the first to break the silence. Speaking slowly, he asked incredulously:

'Have I got this right, Olive? You're proposing to have us sleeping out on Scafell? Under boulders?'

'That's exactly what I am proposing, Mr Birch.' came the reply. 'I realise it won't appeal to everyone, of course, but I think that those of us whose spirit of adventure is not dead, will find it an exciting prospect.'

'Let's get down to the nitty-gritty, Olive,' called Bert. 'What about all the extra weight we'd have to carry? I don't fancy shivering all night and I do like a good fry-up for breakfast. You haven't got porters lined up to carry all the gear, have you?'

'No I have not,' replied O.L., showing signs of irritation. 'We shall be entirely self-sufficient. All you'll need is a duvet sleeping bag together with the space blanket and survival bag which I assume you always carry. As for your fry-up, I think you could do without that for once. I can't imagine Mr Wainwright frying bacon and eggs up there while he was watching the sun rise.'

Harry, initially shell-shocked by O.L.'s idea of sleeping rough, now returned to the attack.

'So what you're saying is that we stagger up to Hollow Stones, wherever that is, laden like pack-horses, find a boulder, supposedly draught-free to spend the night in, wake up – if we ever get any sleep that is – at some unearthly hour and do without a decent breakfast: just to watch the sun-rise! I suppose you imagine a clear moon-lit night. I wouldn't want to bet on that: it's more likely to be wet and cloudy, in which case you'd never see the sun. Your Mr Wainwright doesn't say how many miserable nights he spent under a boulder before he struck lucky with the weather. Frankly, I think it's a crazy idea. You'd have to be a masochist to even think about it'.

O.L. had expected opposition from Harry. Unruffled and smiling sweetly, she replied that any other response from Mr Birch would have surprised her and, no doubt, everyone else. They all knew how much he enjoyed his creature comforts. She went on:

'Of course, it's a gamble with the weather; it always is. But let us not forget the words of Mr Wainwright who said there's no such thing as bad weather, just inadequate clothing. Now let me present you with some facts. I propose we drive up to Wasdale Head on the Saturday afternoon, arriving about 5 o'clock. After a substantial meal at the inn, we set off on the Scafell path for Hollow

Stones. This involves a progressive climb of about 750 metres that most of us will have no problem with. If we leave the inn at 6, we should get there comfortably by 8.30 and set up camp.'

When O.L. paused, anticipating queries, it was Gladys who broke the silence. What worried her in particular was the sleeping accommodation. How many of these draught-free boulders were there and how many people would each one accommodate.

O.L. brushed aside the question. She didn't know for certain how many and how big the shelters were but she was sure they would manage. That was all part of the adventure, not knowing where you were going to lay your head. At this Gladys pulled a face. She hadn't done anything like that since her time in the Girl Guides more than fifty years ago. Besides, her back was used to a spring mattress and would certainly play up if she slept on the ground. Maybe she would leave the adventure to the younger members.

Bert said he didn't mind sleeping rough: his main concern was food and drink. If a proper breakfast was out of the question, he would bring a supply of bacon butties but what about brewing up? He couldn't do without a brew before turning in and first thing in the morning.

O.L. had an answer to this. She, Mike and Joe all had Globetrotter cookers which would provide all the tea they would need. As for bacon butties, she fully approved, adding that she herself would bring a supply of packet soups which they could easily heat up in mugs. Hot soup would be very welcome at 6.30 in the morning when the sun was rising and would sustain them on their subsequent walk up to Scafell Pike and back down to Wasdale via Piers Gill.

O.L.'s casual reference to Scafell Pike came as a surprise, even to Harry.

'So after a sleepless night, up at crack of dawn and packet soup for breakfast, you think we'll feel like climbing Scafell Pike,' he exclaimed, 'you must be joking!'

'Really, Mr Birch,' she replied acidly, 'I can't think why you keep saying 'we.' You surprised us all by getting as far as Black Sail Pass when we went to Pillar and by walking down from Snowdon but I can't for the life of me imagine you spending a night outdoors, much less climbing Scafell Pike. Now, if I may continue! After we've seen the sun light up Scafell Crag, we can be on our way by 7.30. It would be quite unthinkable to miss out on the Roof of England when it's only an hour's walk away. At that time, we'll have it all to ourselves.

'I think you should mention, Olive,' interposed Mike, 'that the path up to Mickledore is over scree and very steep and it doesn't get much better from there up to the top.'

O.L. thanked Mike for this information but she thought they would be fresh and besides, a brisk climb would be ideal to get the blood circulating if it was a chilly morning.

'Which it certainly will be,' added Harry, grinning at Bert, 'though maybe when you're sleep-walking, you don't feel the cold.'

O.L.'s patience was now wearing thin. She told Harry curtly that she had had enough of his negative comments and she sincerely hoped they hadn't put anyone off.

Mavis was the first to reassure her. No, Harry had not put her off. She knew him well enough by now: he just enjoyed stirring things up. She herself thought it would be fun sleeping under a boulder. Seeing the first rays of the sun light up Scafell Crag would be magical and getting to the top of Scafell Pike would be, for her, the icing on the cake.

O.L. beamed. She could not have put it better herself. When there were nods and cries of 'Hear Hear,' she called for a show of hands and counted ten members who were interested. True, they weren't all what she considered strong walkers. Penny and Mavis would slow the pace down but they were what she called 'cheerful plodders' who always got there in the end. She was relieved to hear Gladys say she wouldn't be joining them: never sure-footed at the best of times, at long last she was coming to terms with her age and limitations. As for Harry Birch, she had never expected to be lumbered with him but it was a relief not to see his hand raised. Still, you never knew with that man. She recalled with a grimace how he'd tricked her by taking the train to the top of Snowdon. At least, he couldn't get up Scafell Pike that way.

Betty, inspired by her friend Mavis, had raised her hand after a moment's hesitation but she was concerned about the sleeping arrangements. O.L.'s airy reply to Gladys had done nothing to reassure her. What if they couldn't find enough overhanging boulders to provide shelter for ten people? The prospect of having to walk back to Wasdale Head in the dark was worrying. Joe, who had had similar thoughts, came up with a solution.

'In my opinion,' he said, 'we ought to have a contingency plan. Both Mike and I have two-man tents. Suppose we took them as a back-up? You could take yours as well, Olive, if you don't mind the extra weight.'

'Of course I don't mind the extra weight,' replied O.L. sharply, 'it won't be the first time I've carried a tent on my back. But I won't sleep in it. I'll do what Mr Wainwright did and find a suitable boulder: what's good enough for Mr Wainwright is good enough for me. If Joyce and Mavis prefer to use it, they're welcome.'

When this generous offer was gladly accepted, Harry, who had pricked up his ears at the mention of tents, said that he was now tempted to join them if Joyce and Mavis could find room for him in their tent. Not giving them time to reply O.L. pointed out that even in the highly unlikely event of the ladies agreeing to such an unseemly proposal, there was no way her tent could sleep three.

The meeting adjourned with O.L. promising to give each of her group a check-list of what they needed to carry. In addition to sleeping bag, space blanket and survival bag, they would need basic toilet requisites, food for breakfast and picnics, a torch, gloves and, of course, gaiters and waterproofs. Lingmell Beck would provide them with water and a thermos flask could be useful as could a camera to catch the sun lighting up Scafell Crag. She, Mike and Joe would bring tents and stoves.

As they were leaving, Mavis had a quiet word with Harry.

'It won't be the same without you, Harry, there'll be no-one to keep a rein on O.L. She might have us going up Lord's Rake before breakfast. Any chance of a change of mind?'

'Not the faintest, Mavis my dear,' replied Harry.'I'm not, as you know, one of Wainwright's 'keen fell-walkers.' O.L. and he are birds of a feather, masochists both of them. Mind you,' he went on after a pause, 'I did enjoy the inn at Wasdale Head when you went up to Pillar with Mike and there are some brilliant photo opportunities round about. Maybe I'll go up after all. But not to spend all night shivering under a boulder or in a tent, thank you very much. I'll think about it.'

In the event, Harry did think about it and when Gladys said she'd quite like to go with him 'just for the ride,' he readily agreed and booked two rooms at the inn. O.L. was none too pleased to learn of this arrangement. She envisaged him making facetious remarks at the inn before their departure, weakening morale and undermining her leadership. She would have been happier if he'd stayed at home.

Harry's arrival at the car park on the day of departure, caused a sensation. Wearing a light blue blouson over a white polo-necked sweater, grey check trousers and two-tone brogues, he looked more kitted out for a day at the races than for Wasdale Head. There were ribald remarks from Bert, murmurs of approval from Mavis and a withering glance from O.L. who, nevertheless, was relieved to see that he wasn't going to be walking in that get-up.

Gathering the group round her, she wanted to know if everyone had ticked off all the items on the check-list. Harry's suggestion that an army style kit inspection might be a good idea was met by a stony glare from O.L. and a vehement rejection from Bert who said it had taken him a good hour to pack his rucksack and he wasn't going to do it again for all the tea in China.

'Talking of tea,' said Harry, 'you haven't forgotten the sugar for your early morning brew at 6 o'clock, have you? And what about the tomato sauce for your bacon butties, have you remembered that?'

'We've no time to waste on frivolous banter,' barked O.L., giving Bert no time to reply. 'If everyone is sure nothing essential has been forgotten, we'll be off. Oh, one more thing. The weather forecast for tonight is quite promising: mainly clear skies with some light cloud and the possibility of ground frost in sheltered areas.'

Harry and Gladys were the first to arrive at the inn. By the time the others turned up, they had found their rooms, deposited their bags and were inspecting the menu. The bar was filling up with walkers, some exhilarated and boisterous, some exhausted and subdued, most of them in need of a wash and brush up and all of them hungry and thirsty. Harry, in his immaculate attire, could hardly have been more conspicuous but his appearance only caused a few stares: he was obviously an interloper who had strayed from the residents' lounge.

Much to O.L.'s annoyance, it took some time for all the group to queue up and get served. She had advised them to have a substantial meal but she hadn't bargained for Bert's double helping of chips with his Cumberland sausage, two fried eggs, beans, tomatoes and three slices of bread, followed by apple pie and custard then a wedge of gateau, washed down by countless mugs of tea. Mike and

Joe ran him close and it was not till 6.15 that they were finally ready to leave.

The weather had turned cool but the sun was still shining as Harry and Gladys walked with them along the road until they met the path. Almost tearful, Gladys told the group that she was now sorry to have chickened out. O.L. said they would miss her but assured her it was for the best, adding, as an afterthought, Mr Birch too, of course. Harry smiled and returned the compliment but Bert thought these mutual expressions of regret lacked conviction and muttered to Gladys, 'Miss each other? Those two? Like toothache!'

At the parting of the ways, Harry begged leave to say a few words.

'I would like to wish you all, ladies and gentlemen, 'bon voyage', fine weather and a good night's sleep. I can assure you my thoughts will be with you tonight when I switch off my electric blanket and get into bed. The thought of you all suffering from hypothermia might even prevent me falling asleep. I did toy with the idea of suggesting that you add a hot water bottle to your check-list, Olive, but I didn't think you'd approve – unless, of course, you knew Mr Wainwright used one. Then, in the outdoor shop last week, I came across this.'

With a flourish, Harry produced a small red sachet.

'It says here 'For continuous warmth any time … anywhere. Keeps you warm up to 12 hours.' All you have to do is open the package, remove the pad and shake gently. I've got one for each of you.'

As he distributed the sachets, Harry was rewarded by kisses from all the ladies except O.L. who viewed such familiarity with distaste but who nonetheless gave him a smile, saying it was very thoughtful of him. Harry graciously bowed in acknowledgement.

Leaving Harry and Gladys to walk back to the inn, the group set off at a brisk pace to cross the footbridge over Lingmell Beck and begin the progressive climb up to the rushing torrent of Lingmell Gill. Here, O.L. made sure everyone had full water bottles and she, Mike and Joe filled the extra plastic containers they had brought with them. Everyone was told not to waste a drop. Water for washing was low on the list of priorities: the important thing was to have enough for tea and soup.

As the path steepened up Brown Tongue, Joyce and Penny, oblivious to the grandeur of the mountain scenery ahead, began to lag behind. Mike dropped back to give them moral support leaving O.L. to stride on, apparently unperturbed by all the extra weight she was carrying. Not far behind her came Joe and Syd, both strong walkers. Some thirty yards back, Bert, Bill, Mavis and Betty plodded on grimly.

The sun had disappeared and it was distinctly chilly by the time they all reached Hollow Stones and regrouped. Ahead of them the path levelled out to reveal a grassy area strewn with rocks and boulders of all shapes and sizes, overshadowed by the towering cliffs of Scafell on the right and Pikes Crag on the left with the Mickledore Gap in the middle.

O.L. announced that it was now time to look for the overhanging boulders referred to by Mr Wainwright, ideally one big enough for Mike and Joe to share and two others for Syd and herself. They would then pitch the three tents nearby for Mavis and Joyce, Betty and Penny, Bert and Bill.

The overhanging boulders were not immediately obvious and the light was fading before O.L. pronounced herself satisfied with the three proposed by Mike and Joe for her inspection. When Joyce peered into them, she couldn't repress a shudder and thanked O.L., rather too profusely, for the use of her tent.

'What on earth did you expect?' snapped O.L. 'all mod cons? Now I suggest you and Mavis help Mike and Joe to get the tents up. When everybody's unpacked and made up their beds, we'll get some water boiling for the soup.'

After briskly removing stones and sheep-droppings, O.L. wasted no time getting herself organised. Camera and torch for the sunrise were placed on one side of her bedding, food and water on the other. Her rucksack would serve as a pillow or, if need be, to put her feet in. The stoves were placed outside and while the water was being heated, she felt duty bound to call on the others, offering advice, encouragement and the occasional rebuke. Bert's tent she described as a shambles.

Standing round under a star-lit sky and stamping their feet to keep warm, they gave full marks to the packet soup. O.L. felt well pleased with herself. Everything had gone according to plan so far. The morale of her troops was high and providing the sky remained clear, Scafell Crag would be lit up at dawn in all its glory. Her euphoria was dampened when Mavis said she wondered what Harry would be up to just then.

'Chatting up some bimbo in the bar, I shouldn't wonder,' said Bert.

'We've better things to think about than the doings of Mr Birch,' replied O.L. tartly, 'Just look at that sky! Anyway, I think we should all get to bed. We'll be up at crack of dawn and we've quite a strenuous climb after that to reach Scafell Pike. I wish you all a very good night.'

At least it didn't rain and there was no wind to speak of but it was very cold. With Joyce already in her sleeping bag, wearing everything except boots and anorak, Mavis zipped down the door. The sachet which Harry had given her took a while to generate enough heat to defrost her feet but it was better than nothing. Joyce warned her that she would almost certainly have to get up during the night but would be as quiet as possible.

Bert didn't hear Joyce stumbling around about midnight but he and Bill did hear snoring, It was a low rumbling sound that built up to a crescendo then suddenly exploded with a whistle like an old steam engine.

'That's Syd,' he told Bill, 'He could snore for Wales, that one.'

'If I'd known that,' replied Bill, 'I'd have brought my ear-plugs.'

They weren't alone to suffer from Syd's snoring. Joe reckoned it would be heard 100 yards away. Just as everyone was dozing off during interludes, it would start again. Unable to sleep, O.L. kept looking at her watch, hoping it was time to get up. Mr Wainwright had said time would drag and that was presumably without anyone snoring under a boulder five yards away from him.

At 6 o'clock, O.L. crawled out, not overly surprised to find the ground white. So there had been a frost as forecast. There were wisps of cloud in the sky which was now beginning to lighten but she was sure the sun would break through. No need for reveille: she could hear voices and giggles from all around. But no snoring. Syd was still in the land of Nod, sleeping like a baby. In a loud voice, she announced that tea would be served in five minutes.

Joyce was first in the queue, rubbing her eyes and yawning.

'Not looking your best this morning Joyce,' called Bert.

'You're no oil painting yourself.' she retorted. 'With that woolly balaclava, you look like Compo in Last of the Summer Wine.'

When Syd emerged, looking comparatively refreshed, Bill asked if he'd slept well.

'Not bad at all,' said Syd, 'you don't get any traffic noise up here, do you?'

'Very true,' replied Bill straight-faced, 'it's a haven of peace and quiet,'

Further discussion of the subject was cut short by a shout from O.L.

'It's coming! Look, it's coming! Get your cameras.'

The first rays of the sun had just appeared and were beginning to light up the jagged skyline of Scafell Crag. Scurrying over stones and slipping on the frosty ground, everyone looked for the best vantage point from which to take photos. As more and more of the crag was transformed from black to rosy pink, there were shouts of delight from all directions. O.L. was ecstatic.

'Magic,' she exclaimed, 'pure magic. Something we'll never forget.'

As they were retracing their steps back to the camp-site, Mike noticed that the earlier wisps of cloud had thickened but he said nothing, not wanting to put a damper on the group's high spirits.

O.L. brewed more tea for them to take back to their tents and boulders where it was marginally warmer to eat breakfast. But first, she wanted to say a few words. Seeing the sun rise on Scafell Crag was brilliant but another treat awaited them, Scafell Pike, the Roof of England. The climb up to Mickledore would soon warm them up. They should be ready to leave at 07.30.

So far, they had been lucky with the weather but during breakfast, cloud had settled on Mickledore and it was drizzling. Mike was just about to have a word with O.L. about the advisability of going on, when a cry for help rang out. Mavis was waving her arms near some rocks twenty yards away. Rushing to join her, they found Joyce lying on the ground unconscious. She had gone to relieve herself and when she hadn't returned after several minutes, Mavis had gone looking for her. It seemed as if she'd slipped and hit her head on a rock.

Mike took charge. As a retired policeman he had dealt with situations like this before. There was a bruise on her forehead but no bleeding; no bones broken either, as far as he could judge. But her left foot was sticking out at an abnormal angle. The first priority was to keep her warm. Mike decided they should carry her back to the tent. He knew moving her involved a risk but to leave her in the open, cold and exposed to the rain until help arrived, was even more risky.

In the tent, wrapped in two sleeping bags, Joyce

came round. She had a head-ache and her left foot was painful. It was clear that she would be unable to walk back down to Wasdale Head. Mike dialled 999 on his mobile and asked for 'police' who would then contact Mountain Rescue. He gave his mobile number, the map reference of their position in Hollow Stones and described Joyce's condition. Whether she should be stretchered down or air-lifted was finally up to Mountain Rescue but Mike could give his opinion.

Mike discussed the pros and cons with the group. It would take a stretcher party two hours to get up from Wasdale Head and longer to get down. An ambulance would then be needed to take Joyce to the hospital in Whitehaven. Set against this, a helicopter might take only an hour to reach them and would be able to fly straight to the hospital. Of the two, air-lifting would clearly be the better option.

'I think you've got to abort Scafell Pike, Olive,' said Joe. 'Even without the accident to Joyce, it would be foolhardy to go up in conditions like these.'

O.L. hated admitting defeat but agreement with Joe was unanimous and she nodded glumly. Mike saw no point in the whole group waiting for help to arrive. Suppose Joe and himself stayed with Joyce while O.L. led the others down to Wasdale Head the same way they had come up. They would have to take it slowly to avoid any more falls. O.L nodded but said they would wait until the call from Mountain Rescue came through.

When the call came, Mike repeated the information he'd given the police. The patient had been concussed. She was now conscious, had a headache but was unable to put weight on her injured foot which was causing considerable pain. In his opinion, the sooner she got to hospital the better. A helicopter would have no difficulty landing near where their tent was pitched. He and a friend would wait with the lady until it arrived. The other seven members of the party would make their own way back to Wasdale Head.

Mike gave a thumbs up sign to the others who told Joyce not to worry, she would be air-lifted to hospital. Her main worry, she said, was the bother she was causing but O.L. told her not to be silly. An accident like that could happen to anyone. She herself had slipped on Crib Gogh and was lucky to get away with a sprained ankle. She thought an x-ray of Joyce's foot would be taken at the hospital in Whitehaven. If they then decided she could be treated nearer home, somebody would come and collect her.

Just an hour before, everyone had been elated. Now, the mood was sombre as they packed up, said their good-byes to Joyce, Mike and Joe and set off in silence.

As they made their way down Brown Tongue, measuring every step, the noise of a helicopter overhead relieved the tension and everyone cheered. When the tip of Wastwater came into view after Lingmell Gill had been crossed, Bert cried,

'Only about an hour now. I could murder a pint. I wonder if the bar's open. If it is, I bet Harry's propping it up.'

'Do you think he'll have realised that the turn in the weather has made us give up on Scafell Pike? asked Penny. 'If he hasn't, he won't expect to see us till tea-time.'

'Harry wouldn't expect O.L. to give up because of a

change in the weather,' whispered Mavis. 'Anyway, the rain's stopped and it looks quite bright down there. It wouldn't surprise me if he and Gladys aren't intending to meet us coming down from Piers Gill.'

At that precise moment, Harry was not propping up the bar in the inn. Nor were Gladys and he walking up the Sty Head path to meet them coming down from Piers Gill. They were, in fact, walking up to meet them coming down from Hollow Stones.

O.L. was the first to spot them.

'I can't believe it,' she exclaimed, 'Those two coming up. It's Gladys and Harry Birch!'

'Morning one and all,' shouted Harry. 'Trust you had a good night's sleep.'

'How did you know we'd be coming down this way?' asked Mavis.

'Very useful bit of gear, this' replied Harry, producing his mobile phone, 'Mike told me. He told me about Joyce as well. We saw the helicopter going to pick her up. Now how do you fancy a coffee?'

Gladys and Harry poured coffee from their flasks into plastic cups scrounged from the inn. Sugar, milk and packets of biscuits were also on offer.

'Well, this is a pleasant surprise.' cried Penny. 'Don't you think so, Olive?'

O.L. smiled as if she really meant it and agreed without hesitation. Harry's first pleasant surprise had been giving them those heat sachets on their way up and now here he was providing them with coffee and biscuits on their way down. Her thoughts were expressed by Mavis:

'He has his uses, does our Harry, bless him.'

Back at the inn, to everyone's surprise, O.L. was seen chatting amiably with Harry. She was enthusing about seeing the sun rise on Scafell Crag and showing him the photos she'd taken on her digital camera. Harry could show some of them at his camera club if he would like to. Harry graciously accepted her offer, said they would make a big impression and could he get her a drink. Overhearing this, Mavis whispered to Bert:

'Just look at them. They must have signed a truce. They're like long-lost buddies.'

'Never thought I'd live to see the day,' said Bert, 'It won't last, mind you, they'll be squabbling again at the next meeting, you can be sure.'

When Mike and Joe joined them, Mike rang the hospital. As they suspected, Joyce had broken a bone in her foot but a temporary dressing could be applied if transport was available to get her to a hospital near home.

When Harry at once volunteered to collect her, he went up in O.L.'s estimation for the third time that weekend.